THE SHOCKING TRUE STORY OF A WOMAN'S DECEPTION AND A M...

BURNT

J. D. WATT
2ND EDITION

Dedication

For my family and friends – thank you for your love and
support during this tumultuous time in my life.

For anyone who has experienced the loss, heartache and grief that comes from a relationship ended through deception and broken trust. May you have the courage to live and the confidence to find love again.

Contents

DEDICATION

THE HARBOUR CITY 1

CYBER DATE 6

TAHITI JAMES 15

DESTINATIONSYDNEY 35

TYING UP LOOSE ENDS 51

DESTINATION: SINGAPORE 67

SETTLING IN SYDNEY TOWN 71

MEET THE FAMILY 83

THE EX 91

MEET THE SHERMANS 101

STEPPING UP 107

HAPPY 5TH MONTH ANNIVERSARY 115

TIS THE SEASON 119

STORAGE 129

DEPARTURE TAKE 133

MERRY CHRISTMAS!! 143

YOU'RE WHERE? WITH WHO?! 149

SLOW DEATH 163

THE EXPLANATION 169

JUMPING HURDLES 173

THE DRAGON LIVES 177

LOST... 189

DINNER 195

THE IPAD 207

LILIANFELS 211

HAPPY AUSTRALIA DAY 221

THE 'CONFERENCE' 227

DESTINY.. 237

LATER THAT AFTERNOON 245

THE SET UP.. 245

NO MAN'S LAND 251

PRISONER EXCHANGE 257

TREATMENT 259

SECOND CHANCE?... 272

GOODBYE 286

ABOUT THE AUTHOR 290

ACKNOWLEDGEMENT... 291

ONE

19th July – Day 1

The Harbour City

I had no idea that evening what was going to unfold. I had been invited to drinks by some friends for my birthday, at a 'secret venue'. All very mysterious but I needed an outing. I had just ended a very bad relationship with a woman who had fallen madly in love with my wallet and not my heart. I was so happy to end it but was still feeling a bit bruised and I thought this night out would be just the tonic.

So off I went with my friends Liz and Jeremy. I had been introduced to them on my ferry by another mutual friend, and before long we had generated a commuter friendship which ultimately crossed over into a social relationship.

Their daughter Carly would often be on the boat and before long we would engage in banter which usually consisted of me regaling them with the amorous adventures of a middle-aged bachelor. Jeremy was a dour, six foot four Italian and Liz a bubbly Greek. Carly was a perfect fusion of the two, carrying the height gene, towering over most people. This of course was the primary source of her concern.

"I need a tall guy!!"

"Really?" I questioned sarcastically. I suggested she hang out with basketballers.

It was eventually revealed that the mystery adventure was going to be 'Tango Night' at the Crystal bar. This bar is located in the Westin Hotel and I had been there many times. It was a sophisticated, up-market venue and usually had a clientele mix of

1

business suits and party people.

'Tango Night' meant that every 30 minutes after 8pm, a professional Tango couple would perform amongst the patrons, whirling in and out of the groups and generally providing a quite unique form of entertainment. I was bemused. We were enjoying the atmosphere and the music and I met a number of Liz's friends who had also been invited.

At about 9.30pm Carly arrived with some of her friends. I asked her how she was and before long we were enmeshed in the usual discussion ...BOYS!! Like most modern young women, her constant companion in life had become her iPhone, and she was texting and talking at the same time. I expressed my annoyance at this habit and suggested if she really wanted to meet someone we should attempt the old fashioned method of actually talking to people!

"And guess what? We are in a bar full of people, and it just so happens to be your good fortune to be with one of the best wing men in the game!" I said with complete modesty. So I dared her to join me in a full frontal attack on the opposite sex, right there, right now! She took some considerable coaxing but finally agreed.
"So, let the games begin" I stated ceremoniously.

I had no idea what universal forces would be unleashed, and this is the beginning of my tale.......

"Carly, let me show you how to cruise a bar." So we walked from one end to the other, pausing and observing. She had said she wanted a tall man, so we went giant hunting. Admittedly the specimens available were not all that encouraging. However we finally walked past a group of people and, low and behold a giant! I looked at her as she saw him, and I noticed her giving him the laser gaze assessment, then her eyes flicked to me with a smile.
"Yep he is cute. So what do we do now?" I looked at her with the re- assuring wisdom of an old pro and said, "It's so simple, I will go over and introduce myself. I will be your cousin and I will see if he

would like to join us for a drink."

She looked at me with cynical disbelief. I turned and walked over towards the giant's nest. The rest was simple; I had done it many times. Luckily I am charming and have a sense of fun and could easily inject myself into a group of strangers. So I broke the ice and asked the tall fellow, who introduced himself as Dale, if he would like to join my cousin and I for a drink? I added that she thought he was cute, so he would know that this was a set up.

"Sure bring her over and we will buy her a drink." Dale said with a smile.

Before long I had a group of new friends all laughing and enjoying the moment. I had assessed that they were decent chaps, and there was a woman amongst the group so it would not be completely intimidating for Carly.

Carly came over and with introductions made, the banter commenced. We had a drink and a laugh and Carly couldn't believe that she had met a tall stranger at a bar. I could sense that the moment was passing so I thanked them for their hospitality and we started to walk back to her parents and our party.

Carly was clearly buoyed by the experience and was feeling as though she had achieved a milestone, that moment of simple interaction with a real man, and it had nothing whatsoever to do with social media!

"Michael that was so much fun, thank you. Now I will find you someone." She turned around and began to survey the room. I thought, well I'm really not interested at the moment but ok, let's have some fun!

"What about that blonde over there?" Carly pointed towards someone. "the one in the leather jacket?"

I strained to see who she was talking about but there were too many people in the way. She was already making a beeline towards her.

"Hold on, I need to see her first Carly." So I maneuvered between a few people and finally caught a glimpse of Simone.

I think I noticed her eyes first. They were sad. She seemed so vulnerable. It was curious that I thought this, but it would be a constant theme in our short-lived friendship. Carly introduced us, and Simone introduced her friends.

She was out with her best friend Peta and her good friend Donald, and another boy who made no impression. By their admission they had been drinking for hours and were all pretty animated, but somehow Simone and I just stood there, looking at each other and staring into each other's eyes. I thought I had better start the conversation.

"So, tell me" I said, "what is your situation?" She answered and I immediately detected an Italian accent.

"I have just come back from Singapore. I broke up with my partner 3 months ago and I am going to live here now." Somehow when she told me this, I felt a surge of adrenalin and with it... extraordinary energy.

"Well funny that... I just broke up with my girlfriend too." She smiled and we launched into a discussion.

She had been in Singapore for two years and couldn't stand the climate and the crowds. She had lived with Marco the 'ex' for two years in Australia. He had taken a Singapore posting to advance his career.

We talked and laughed. Time stopped. Then I was thrown into shock. She told me that she was flying back to Singapore tomorrow and this was her farewell party. I asked her when she would be back and she told me that she would be packing her things and would return in about a month. Oh well, I thought, that wasn't that long to wait, if indeed this introduction had any possibilities.

"Shall we have dinner when you get back?" she laughed and said she would love to. With that encouragement, we exchanged details and then I suggested we head back to our respective parties. We smiled at each other and it was electric; we had an instant attraction and connection.

I saw Jeremy approaching out the corner of my eye. "We thought we had lost you, ah but I see you have been distracted" he said wryly. I think Jeremy has an eye for pretty girls and this was a good excuse to see what I was up to.

"This is Simone from Rome." His eyes lit up and he immediately broke into Italian, exchanging pleasantries for a few minutes.

We then bid her farewell, and as we watched her disappear into the crowd, Jeremy turned to me and with a broad grin and a wink,

"Roman girls are the best!!" he stated with enthusiasm.

I felt elated. Fate had brought me to a new venue and presented a beautiful blonde haired, green eyed beauty right before me. I knew it wasn't one sided. She had made it very clear she was interested in me too. I was somewhat overwhelmed and didn't feel like being ensconced in a loud bar anymore. I wanted to be alone with my thoughts, so I decided that I would bid my friends good-bye and head home. After thanking my hosts I turned for the door and there she was again. I went over and said how wonderful it was to meet her, and I would stay in touch.

In the taxi home, I could not stop thinking about her. In fact she was the only thing I was thinking about. And with her on my mind that evening I fell into a deep peaceful slumber.

TWO

20th July Day 2

Cyber Date

There is certain energy that one feels when Cupid's arrow hits its mark. At first I thought that it could only be a casual meeting at a bar. A girl who would go back to Singapore and then we would forget about each other. But no, this girl was embedded in my thoughts and I felt great. I was back up on the bike so soon after falling off.

The next day I sent an email to her wishing her a great flight and hoping that we would catch up in Sydney when she returned. I didn't know whether she would reply, but nothing ventured, nothing gained, and low and behold her response arrived almost immediately, and from that moment on, we began to correspond on a regular basis. It was a bit like having an old-fashioned pen-friend, only the responses were almost immediate. The messages were light and fun with a touch of cheekiness. I suggested that I would like to ask her on a cyber-date.

"Let's Skype", I suggested. She returned fire with a message that was quite strange.

"Where are you with your life?" she enquired. She said that I had told her the night we met, that I was married with two children! She was not in the habit of having Skype dates with married men. I assured her that she must have met someone else that night, because I was divorced with one child. So we set a time and agreed to talk. About this time, we started texting, a habit usually associated with Generation Y, but one which I comfortably slipped into.

5 August

> Hi Simone guess who downloaded the wrong app?? Carly my wing woman saved me!!!
> 4.46pm

> Haha, Always handy to have a smart woman around I say!
> Say hi to Carly and thank her for rescuing you from the evils of modern technology
> 4.51pm

> Yes … I have to admit … Technology is not my bag... That's why I need a smart woman!! If u get back too late tonight let's make a time tomorrow?? I'm off to the gym. M x
> 5.01pm

> Enjoy the gym, work on those guns and I'll let you know if I'm home earlier than expected. Otherwise tomorrow!
> 5.26pm

I left it at that, and immediately went to test my Skype connection as it had not been used for quite a while, and as if fate was conspiring against me, I was right, the damn thing had packed up and was not working. I was gripped by panic! I am not a tech person. I need a fall back plan, who has a spare computer? I called a friend of mine, Dominic, who by co-incidence was Italian, and thankfully was young and savvy and completely understood computer technology and was able to diagnose the problem. The camera was not working. So a special trip to the electronics store, a purchase of a new digital camera and suddenly the apparatus came to life. I was saved with one day to spare.

Finally the big day arrived. I realised that I had created all these expectations in my mind. In truth, I couldn't remember exactly what she looked like. I had Googled her and could not find a photo of her. It had been weeks since 'Tango Night' and I felt that I was losing those once vivid memories.

The designated hour arrived; my first official cyber date using Skype. My heart was in my mouth. The dial tone rang, once, twice, and then she answered. She looked lovely. She had bought a bottle of Champagne and I was sipping single malt and we talked...and talked... and talked. Banter inter mixed with an exploration of each other.

I learned that she had split from Marco and had moved into the spare bedroom and couldn't wait to get out of there.

She told me about her childhood in Italy and growing up with an abusive father. All in all we spoke for about two hours. She had managed to sink the entire bottle of bubbles, and I had downed two scotches, which lately was a rarity for me. I used to enjoy indulging in social drinking with colleagues or friends, but recently had made a conscious decision to focus on maintaining my health, so I had cut right back on my alcohol intake.

We said good night and suddenly there was a reality to the fact that we really liked each other and she was coming back. I was elated. I had not felt so good for months. The tempo of our e-mails picked up and she introduced me to a new phone App for free international texting and I took to it like a duck to water. Suddenly we were texting and Skyping regularly. It was almost as if we were dating. It felt good. We were getting to know each other and not just jumping into a physical relationship.

During the course of these first few weeks she told me of her plans in more detail. She had booked a holiday to Tahiti some time back with Marco, but he was no longer relevant so she had invited a girlfriend to go with her. She was also trying to line up some job interviews here so there was a possibility that she would be able to get to Sydney, before her final move.

5 August

I am so excited. Just found out I'm short listed for a job I applied for in Sydney! They requested I send more information today and hopefully I will hear about whether I have made the cut after 16/08 Fingers and toes crossed!!
5.26pm

Hey!! Just saw your message about the position!!! How exciting!! I know that u will get a fantastic position!!! So did u see the movie the Godfather?!! I am going to make u an offer u can't refuse!!!! X
6.24pm

Who hasn't watched the Godfather? Gathering from your reference, I should either be freaked out or be feeling secure that your offer may be rather enticing...lol ???? speak soon... super busy xxx
6.45pm

Hahaha not at all... Tell me when your meeting ends! X"
6.56pm

I've just finished now!! Need to wrap up now and run to meet Sally. I am STARVING, I only had a piece of fruit today and am about to eat the next person that crosses my way!!
8.32pm

U need to have proper food!!! x how was your day??
8.35pm

Super stressful!! Yeah, maybe I should go vego.
I guess I'll have a quick bite now with Sally. She is moving apartments. She already looked at 2 apartments and has had enough. All dirty and disgusting or super expensive.
That's my take on Singapore anyway... Haha
How is your evening tracking along? x
9.21pm

Well I am just settling down to
an episode of the Tudors!!
Love it!! Looking forward to
introducing u to Henry!!
And I'm actually thinking about u
quite a bit x
Tell me I am not crazy
9.23pm

In my mind I certainly don't think
you're crazy... but perhaps I'm
biased!!??
I'm actually enjoying the idea
that you are thinking and texting
me a lot.
You're certainly in my thoughts
too!!!
But I need to focus now on my
friend. xoxo
9.27pm

U must be a good friend.
So lets discuss tomorrow
9.29pm

She says 'Thank You', and I say
goodnight
9.43pm

7 August

Morning!! Chilly but beautiful
day here!!
Ps hard to sleep last night, I was
thinking about u!!
7.43am

11

Well, I couldn't sleep very well either.
I was working late last night with one of the big bosses till well after midnight, and by then I was too wired to sleep.
Tossed and turned all night. Have to say there's a lot going on in my head as well;-)
I've just come up with a super plan. I need to talk to big boss first, but I will volunteer myself to come to Sydney to help set up office for their joint venture....lots of organizing to be done, but given I do so much extra work above and beyond my job description, I think they will concede. Worth a try anyway. Hope your morning is going well? I'll keep you posted! X
9.36am

Excellent thinking 99!! I am sure we will work out something!! X
9.37am

I remember it was a few days before she left for Tahiti that I had received a text from her. Simone was over the moon. She had managed to organise a trip to Sydney for a job interview and would be able to see me. As a result her holiday would be cut in half and she would be flying to Sydney. This meant we could have 5 days together and really get to know each other. I was ecstatic. I couldn't believe that someone was taking the initiative like this. She liked me and was following her heart.

Our texting developed an edge, a sense of urgency, and it was intoxicating. We were both falling for each other and we had only talked to each other in person for 30 minutes, that night at the Crystal Bar.

9 August

I'm calling flight centre this afternoon... Let's see what they come up with! Fingers crossed!
3.00pm

Everything is possible so if u strike a problem I am sure that I will be able to fix it!!! X
3.23pm

I emailed you. It is on, and it is now safe to add...
I'm a nutbag!
Can you believe it??
4.58pm

Why r u crazy?? Am lecturing in an hour.
Sitting in Uni café ... I must be getting old!
These kids.... Was I that young?!!x
5.03pm

I lectured at a local University part time, teaching law to undergraduates. I had been doing this for 13 years and quite enjoyed the interaction with students

I emailed you my details.
Arriving on 21, leaving on 26 ;-)
5.05pm

Arriving in Sydney ?????
5.06pm

No, Hawaii!!!!
5.06pm
Of course Sydney!
5.07pm

Fantastic!! I am so happy!!!!
xxxxxxxx
5.08pm

THREE

9th August - Day 22

Tahiti James

It is a wonderful feeling when you start to feel in step with the spirit of another human being, and this is what was beginning to happen to us. The texting became addictive, along with the Skype calls and of course one's imagination. You begin to slowly move into a world of possibilities and ask the question over and over, is she the one? With. every text there is more familiarity and more urgency. Those funny little face emojis started to appear regularly, lots of winking and blowing kisses. The language of love was now transcending into the digital and cyber world of prefabricated icons.

The days rolled by interminably. My mind often drifted into daydreams of the two of us and a possible future together, only to be jolted by the sudden arrival of more of her texts.

9 August

You are so lovely!!
I feel very close to you and care for you quite a lot, which is a little scary and confusing considering our very brief encounter at the Crystal bar.
9.43pm

I know, but it was great and u were so cute I know it's crazy but that's half the magic....
We have got to know each other the old-fashioned way. Talking and writing letters, albeit with some hi-tech help. But it is special. And I feel it Hope this doesn't scare u!!!xx but I want to be honest, I am thinking about u a lot!!! X Xox
9.46pm

It takes a lot more to scare me Mr!!
Don't be fooled by my small delicate build, I'm not as vulnerable as I look. Lol
I love your honesty!! Not sure what is wrong with people these days but nobody seems to give away how they feel anymore. Probably not cool...
God knows!?!? Don't stop!!! Ok, I'm out of here, all done ... I think! Meeting my friend now, chat later!
9.49pm

Ps: I'm thinking about you a lot as well
Xxxxx
9.53pm

The adventure begins my beautiful little Simi, have a safe flight, and don't drink too much champagne!!
By all means send me some pics!! Xoxoxox M
9.57pm

No worries... Can't promise regarding the champagne;-)) x
Lets not get too excited, we may get bored with each other after a day, or worse, you will think I'm a bore!!!
I will admit I have butterflies in my tummy x
10.03pm

Hahahahaha....
U have butterflies in your tummy??
And u r nervous!! I am not .
I have a great feeling about u!!
What if I bore u ??? xoxo
10.05pm

Never!!! Sweet Dreams
10.06pm

Don't worry we will be great together!!
Hahahahaha...Am going to bed soon so have a wonderful flight!!
xoxo
10.06pm

She arrived on the island and settled into a routine of sun, surf, beach and swimming. I received regular updates and photos. One in particular was quite charming. She had gone swimming with dolphins. There is something about dolphins that always warms the heart. Blue skies, crystal clear water and a beautiful blonde in a bikini swimming with a pod of dolphins. The image was perfect. I had half a mind to jump on a plane and put myself in a few photos alongside her. But I knew she would be here in less than six days and counting...

13th August

> Hi again, when u read this I am sure I will be asleep, so I thought I would tell u that I have been thinking about u and wondering what sort of person u r. Of course I think I have gotten to know u quite well, and I think that u r just lovely!! But I really want to get to know u and hear all about your life. I want you to tell me about your childhood, your schools, your first loves, what u hope for? what u dream about? Sounds a bit schmaltzy?? Well I am interested in u little Simi, so don't type it all ... Just think about it so u can tell me in person...speak soon Xoxo M
> 4.39pm

Once again I wake up to beautiful words.
Thank you!!! I'm blessed that you express so much interest in me!! I think I can honestly say I am just as interested in you and have many questions myself so be prepared!
Fingers crossed our political and religious views aren't too opposing...lol. We have so much to discuss and learn about one another. I am more than happy to tell you all about my life, dreams and hopes!! but excuse me in advance as I may get

embarrassed, no-one has ever taken the time to ask me to indulge them with my life's stories. I appreciate your interest.
It makes our union even more exciting. I love it here. I almost had a perfect day before I cut my foot on some coral when I jumped off my Paddle board. Luckily the local surf shop had all the right disinfecting solutions. So should be healed by the time I'm in Sydney with you next week. BTW, my phone is playing up again which is extremely annoying!! The round centre button doesn't work anymore which makes it extremely difficult to go from app to app. So contact might be a bit sporadic over the next few day. I hope you had a good start to the week?!
7.10am

Even though I'm home earlier today, I trust you must be in bed by now. Sweet dreams! I'm heading down for a dip in the water at the beach just around the corner from my house. Speak (text) with you tomorrow!! X
3.30pm

Hello!! Another relaxing day in Paradise!!!
Lying by the beach is the perfect backdrop for me to have some reflection time. Really think about my future once I've moved to Sydney.
It's weird because a few months

ago I was with a man for 6.5 years, and I thought that was my future, and even though the split was the right decision, it still feels weird that I'm now in control of my own destiny, and then out of the blue you show up and now its quite possible that you are my destiny...maybe?!? I'm listening to some music today while sitting by the sea- I love how music takes you back to certain times in your life, and you're able to recall moments so vividly based on a single tune. Or the way the lyrics speak to you so profoundly about love or life in general. Music always helps me, couldn't live without it. One of my fave songs is basically saying that relationships and love are hard work and they constantly require nurturing! Marco never really did and I didn't have the strength to hold it all together myself in the end..."It's a hard life, to be true lovers together, to love and live forever in each others heart..." So true! Sorry, I'm getting a little heavy!!
Must be the sun. I feel like I can tell you anything. Take it as a compliment. Hope you had a great day!?
Still no sunburn here but I'm starting to get those tiny freckles in my face. I quite like them... Makes me look at least 3 months younger. Have a nice evening and sweet dreams later! x thank you!!!
3.35pm

Best medication! Salt water
Hey I am here!!!
And here for u!!! Xoxo
I understand what u r feeling
I wish I could give u a hug!!
I have been where
u r 5 years ago.
Amazing how music can bring
back such strong emotions.
I think we r going to have so
much to talk about!!!! U have to
trust the universe little Simone....
And yourself I know what it
takes to love someone now...
And I understand so completely
your comments about nurturing
love. So lets begin ... The new
journey together xoxo
Heading to bed early myself.
Thanks for sharing your
thoughts.
U can tell me these things. Xx
7.03pm

Then something unexpected happened. She texted me in a semi panic. She couldn't believe it but Marco had turned up out of the blue at her hotel!

15 August

Marco just showed up at
breakfast!!!
Can you believe it!!
He is so arrogant in his thinking.
The audacity. I'm ready to
explode.
We have never had a single fight,
but my blood is boiling. I could
kill him.
I have politely told him to fuck
off and not impede on my time
here. I really needed this holiday
to sort stuff out in my head.

I do not need this extra stress, even though we get on as friends, it's not the point.
I'm so upset!! Text you later.
4.24pm

OMG !! I am so sorry!!
If u need to talk I can call later.
Please don't be upset.
U own the future. ... And he is not in that book... Xoxo
4.25pm

Keep me posted xoxo
4.30pm

R u ok?? I have been worried about u!!
R u able to Skype?
Would u like me to call?
7.25pm

WOW what a day hey? Really, I don't know why I reacted so surprised. That is so typical of how he is. He had already taken the time off when we were together and originally booked the holiday, and he does love surfing, but still, thinking that he could show up and EXPECT to stay with me was just a little TOO much.
Anyway, he got the message. I helped him find somewhere else, and he can take over my room when I come and see you.
He's a mad surfer so prob won't see him much.
Just letting you know we are having dinner tonight.
Just to chat in general. ... so all good over here.
Hope your day was more relaxing....and yes, he is

> definitely not part of my
> future... that book belongs to
> us!! Enjoy your evening!! And
> thanks for caring!!
> Xx
> 7.28pm

She couldn't believe it! She explained he had a habit of doing this sort of thing, but couldn't believe he would have the gall to follow her half way round the world. I couldn't believe it. I felt so hopeless. I even contemplated jumping on a plane and flying to her rescue.

Her text calmed me and assured me that she had had 'the discussion' again with him, the old 'It's over...we are finished...don't you get it?!'. I was somewhat relieved and felt assured she was on the same page as me.

> Back from dinner at the local
> pizzeria.
> Lots of local surfers there, quite
> a relaxed cool vibe, so he will
> have some surfing mates to hang
> with from now on! I explained
> that I have lined up interviews on
> my 5 days in Sydney, and I also
> revealed that I had met an
> amazing man that is slowly
> sweeping me off my feet,
> perhaps it was too soon to let
> him know, he seemed a little
> pissed off. Think he can't handle
> that he has no control over my
> decisions anymore.
> Bedtime for me, it's been a really
> big day emotionally.
> Can't wait to see you in 5 days
> and fingers crossed
> I get a job in Sydney X
> 11.28pm

I settled down, but felt churned inside. Even though it had been ten days since we first texted each other, I couldn't believe how emotionally invested I had become. I truly cared about her. I had that male instinct to protect the vulnerable and Simone was my maiden in distress, 6,000 kilometres away. It had been a long time since I'd had these feelings. And it wasn't easy being so far away from her. In truth, it was I that felt vulnerable, but at the same time, invincible. More re-assuring texts arrived and soon we settled back into the regular pattern of our exchanges.

20 August

> Hi!! Now it's 4 days!!! It's like counting down to a moon launch!! Well we r going to the stars I hope!! Together!! What a ride it will be!! I don't think I have been described as amazing before, but that's fine. I see u in the same light!! And u have beautiful legs!!!! I should let u know, so do I!! But seriously I can say that I have a wonderful feeling about u. And am happy to tell u. I love looking at your pictures. And thinking about u, and don't say that u will bore me etc etc. I know how smart u r, we have talked remember? And u r.... Well I won't say it now but I will certainly tell u when I see u. Let's just say my heart is open, and u have stolen it. I love the feeling of having u in my life!! And if it is this good with Skype, pics and texts ...Imagine when we r together!!!

> So Simi, I hope u r smiling and I hope that this message makes u feel as warm and fuzzy as I feel writing it. BTW, U deserve the best, and that's why the universe introduced us!!! xoxo
> 7.13am

> Beautiful!!!! Still keen for me to come??
> 7.15am

> Hahahaha... No second thoughts at my end little Simi!! Am already planning our time. Will of course confer this evening!!
> 7.17am

> Very sweet of you to make plans for the time already btw, but I'm also trying to squeeze some interviews in and, it is Donald's, birthday on Friday so I hope you are happy to come along for some drinks??
> 7.20am

> Of course I would love to be your date!!! Lets discuss tonight. I don't want to take all your time. But want to do some special things with you and for you!! X
> 7.23am

... three days... two days...

With this phone app you can send a voice message, so I thought I would give it a try. She responded immediately.

19 August

> You put a smile on my face.
> Thank you!!
> Do you know what is funny? How I can miss someone I met for 30 minutes a few weeks ago.
> Yet I feel I really know you and trust you so much.
> Weird!!!! Not long to go now.
> Text me anyway, and I'll respond as soon as I can. I wish I was sitting on a secluded beach with you.
> See you soon. And thanks for the voice message.
> 8.05am

I started to think that she hadn't really told me much about her friend Sally that she was travelling with. All of the photos she had sent through to me were only ever of her out and about on boats, or lying at the beach. This fleeting thought was soon overwhelmed by my total focus on her. My feelings for her were growing daily. My excitement was taking on a new energy. It was hard to fathom that this angel would soon be travelling across the skies and landing on my doorstep...

20 August

> Hey there, finally some time to myself.
> Just put Sal to bed and having a night cap before crashing out.
> Our exhausting conversation was all about her terrible relationship.
> Which makes me think about us. In order for us to have a chance, we need to spend the next 5

days being brutally honest with each other.
I'm ready to be open with any questions you may have for me, and hopefully you will be an open book for me too?
Then you can decide if you like me or not... not that I have massive demons in my cupboard...lol
So do we have a deal? Complete honesty?
5.17am

Morning!! X well one more sleep for us and u will be here!! Yes it's a deal.
Of course I agree. Honesty is the first pillar of a great relationship, second communication. Actually there r many ingredients I really believe from what we have said and written that we share a very similar outlook!! So much to talk about. I have made many mistakes, I am only human. I am ready to share with u. I want us to grow together. I guess we have both set the bar pretty high in the past, I have said to myself that I will not settle for second best and something tells me that with u, that will not be a problem. So don't worry, sit back and relax. U will be in safe hands!!
xoxo
5:41 am

Good morning! Well... It is 3.20am here
And I can't sleep. Sally has completely commandeered the bed and I have been pushed to a tiny corner, so I thought I'd get

up. Yes the bar has been set high, but with the right amount of love and honesty and communication, we have the start of something pretty special. Whether it be a great friendship...or maybe, hopefully something a lot more. We all have made mistakes....it's what makes us human.
So here's to sharing our past and possibly our future together. See you tomorrow!!!
But no doubt we will txt prior to then...lol
5.50am

Hey, go back to sleep!! And dream about me!!! I hope u do set the bar high I have to warn u, I am up for the challenge. Open your heart as I have opened mine and all will be good, and then great ....
And then superb!!
And then sublime!! Xox
6.03am

I am trying!!! Believe me Michael, my heart is wide open so I'm ready for the challenge too! Yes I may be a little nervous, but I think anyone would be...Ok, I will attempt to get another hour of sleep!! Talk later! X
6.05am

Sleep tight ... I am....
Well I will tell u in person!! Xox
6.09am

You are what?? Now I'm curious, And my butterflies are fluttering xx
6.10am

> Hahaha... I knew that would get u. I will send u a voice message ...
> Xx
> 6.11am

I recorded a few thoughts on love and pressed "send".

> My goodness that was lovely!! Unfortunately, I can't record you one back Sally will wonder what I was doing Although I have told her little bits about us, but not the full gamut, because we don't even know that yet. Plus she needs her sleep right now xxxxx
> 6.18am

> What happened to Sally? Broken heart?
> 6.20am

> Good guess Mr Perceptive!!!! Her boyfriend has been cheating on her for 7 months. Can you believe it???
> And to top it off he is paying for an apartment for his mistress... What's wrong with people these days???
> 6.22am

> That's terrible! I value fidelity. Trust is the most important element.
> It is the glue that binds two people together.
> I am so sorry to hear that... X
> She is probably just another gold digger!!
> I know the type!! Sorry for being so judgmental!!
> Makes me cranky!!! X
> 6.30am

29

> Not judgmental. Right on the money!
> They're a dime a dozen hunting down the bearer of a platinum credit card, regardless of what they look like or compatibility.
> Sickening and sad!!!!
> 6.35am

We went about our day knowing that within 24 hours we would be together in the same city. Every message, or email or Skype conversation, seemed to cement our relationship even more.

> Arriving at airport in a minute...
> 6.35pm

> Well do u want to taxi to me?
> And freshen up here? X
> 6.36pm

> Hmm, does sound good.
> Then we could head out for a yummy breakfast.
> How does that sound? If you don't mind?!!
> 6.40pm

> Please don't think that u r imposing!!
> Ur not. In a way u r my guest, so don't think twice about it.
> I can arrange to have u picked up if u would like!!
> Please let me spoil u a little???!!!
> X Just need the flight Number.
> 6.44pm

> No, I can take a regular cab!!!
> You are too sweet.
> I should get a taxi in no time! Ok, through customs already, this is so efficient!!

Checking alcohol restrictions now
Not allowed, sorry!!
7:02 pm

Well my address is Unit 63 / 77 – 79 New South Head Rd, Darling Point. Tell the driver to turn onto New Beach Road, then call me. 0578 244 245 I will guide him. Everyone gets lost it's so simple. Go to the end of New South Head Rd and turn left up the hill. My Building is called Harbour Gardens! I will have your cappuccino on arrival xoxo
7.10pm

Wonderful! Thanks
7.11pm

So just text me when u land xox
7.13pm

Ok! Hey, quick question. Would this work for an interview??
I like to wear things that people remember.
It seemed to work in the past.
7.45pm

She sent me a photo of her in a gorgeous dress. Just like a typical lady, she was killing time at the airport browsing in the designer shops. She took my breath away. She looked divine....and Miss Divine was heading towards me and would be in my arms within hours. It was surreal. How the hell did I get so lucky?!

I will interview u!!!!
U Look stunning! Yes Xox
7.47pm

Thanks, haha!
Want to be my personal zipper-upperer?
7.48pm

I volunteer
7.49pm

Cheers! To us and the days ahead!
7.53pm

Yes cheers to us!! So put your feet up and relax now! And think about life!! Xo
8.13pm

Already doing that. Have I told you how excited I am? LoL yes I do believe I have... life is certainly looking good
8.15pm

Thank you so much for taking a chance, and for backing us and for being prepared to move the world!!! I know u r an amazing woman and I am humbled to have u in my life!! xx
8.19pm

Oh wow, flutter flutter!!
Michael YOU are amazing!!!!
It is because of you that I have taken this chance. We moved the world together.
You made me realize that fate has stepped in and played a part in shaping our future.
You have reignited my passion and now my heart is open and ready. So really, it is I that should be thanking you.... Oh god, I just got super excited again...I can't wait to see you now.

This is such a weird scenario!!!!
Lol
It still freaks me out...but I will
say this....
I like the way you make me feel...
xx
8.24pm

Thank u. U will get to know me,
the funny side and the serious
side.
The serious side says that this is
very important for both of us. I
know it will be wonderful. U
make me feel amazing too!!
Words can't describe that feeling
of warmth just thinking about u.
And as for making u feel the fire?
Simone u r beautiful, not just
your beautiful face, but the
gentleness I sense. I think we
met at a time in our lives that
was perfect ... Xx
8.33pm

I'm sitting in the waiting area
grinning like a Cheshire cat. No
doubt I'm attracting weird looks
from people nearby. I cannot
even remember a time when
anyone has said such beautiful
words. Thank you!!!!
I don't feel special....but lately,
you have been making me feel
super special, and I agree, it does
feel like perfect timing. I guess
we will know one way or the
other over the next week if this is
meant to be or not. Hard to
imagine at this stage that we
wouldn't work....everything
seems to flow so easily. I actually
have goosebumps...
8.40pm

I agree!! As for not being special, let me be the judge!!! I think u r very special. I love goose bumps, LOL I am going to have a shower, so I will text when I am dry!!! Don't have too much champagne!! Xox
8.45pm

OK, although in regards to champers, the host remembers me from previous travels, and keeps topping me up every few minutes.
8:48pm

He probably likes u!!! Xx
8.53pm

No, not at all. Business class is virtually empty, he's probably bored.
Just means I will get quite drunk.... only joking. I'm exhausted and will try and get a good night sleep! Ok really turning phone off now!! Xx
8.55pm

Have a wonderful flight!!! xoxo
8.56pm

Finally she was on her way to Sydney. I couldn't believe it. This beautiful young woman would be arriving ... and sitting next to me in a matter of hours.

FOUR

21st August - Day 33

Destination Sydney

I had decided to take a couple of days leave whilst she was in Sydney. I wanted to spend quality time with her and was looking forward to having a real opportunity to get to know her. I had planned our days together and our nights, and although I had no real expectation that there might be a physical relationship, secretly deep down, I hoped this might be the case. Before she arrived she was contemplating her choices of where she would stay. I thought the choice was obvious......

21 August

I'm now on a mission to find accommodation closer to the CBD. The city would be much more convenient for my job interviews. Plus makes it easier to catch up with people. X
9.10am

Let's discuss this too tonight!! I have a suggestion xx
9.11am

There's always a backpacker hostel for $18 per night!! Awesome!! NOT!!!!
9.12am

I have never slept with a backpacker!!
9.12am

Ok, Mercure is $145 per night. I need to be quick though I reckon as it is a special deal...x
9.15am

Simone If u book there can you cancel without forfeiting any money?
If u were to get a better offer??
9.18am

No it is a special deal.
Still checking other places.
9.19am

Simone I don't want to be presumptuous, and I don't want u to get the wrong impression but, I have room and a spare bed, and I give my word as a gentleman that there will be no...Well u know what I mean, anyway it's an option. I wanted to discuss this with you, and please don't be offended Xx

PS it comes with the most amazing breakfast ... And me!! And I can provide referees X
9.30am

That is so lovely of you, but at this early stage, I think it's important that we maintain a sense of independence, and it also takes the pressure off both

of us. Also, if we don't get on, it's not awkward with any quick exits that might take place....lol.... Please don't be offended and thank you again for the kind offer xx
9.13am

Not offended, I understand completely, but I still reserve the right to romance your socks off!!! xx and we can still have breakfast!!!
Hope u don't get wrong impression. Where is it?? Just checked, it's 10 minutes from me.
9.16am

I know
9.16am

Perfect!!
9.17am

Romance my socks off?!
Haha, sounds interesting, I am looking forward to that...!! x
9.20am

I had booked opera tickets and thought we could also drive to the mountains for a day. I envisaged long walks in some quaint country town, and a chance to talk about our lives. All the classical ingredients tossed together for romance. I would give it my best shot. Who knows it might actually work.

I had been single for some five years now and felt like I had dated every psychotic woman in Sydney. How that many nutters could live in one community of single women defied explanation. I had had a number o relationships but once the romance turned to reality, they had all fallen apart. Was it me? I think not. Well I hoped not anyway.

I have a great group of friends and emotional support from the two finest women I have ever known, my ex-wife and my daughter. I had grown over the last five years. I had matured as a man, and knew what I wanted, because I had seen so much of what I didn't want. I realised that often, so often, beauty was skin deep and that so few women offered the qualities that I desired. I was by no means perfect either, but I really felt that I had now got my head together and was for the first time in my life feeling, as they say, comfortable in my own skin. I actually hate that expression. After all, who else's skin would I be in??

I truly felt that if things were meant to happen they would. I had taken the pressure from myself and after all, that's how we had met. It was organic not contrived. So with these thoughts rushing through my head the text that I had been waiting for weeks, the text that seemed to re- affirm the reality that had now befallen me, hit my phone.

21 August

> I have arrived!!! I'm outside your building. xx
> 7.17am

A shot of adrenalin rushed through my body. I took a deep breath, exhaled and felt a profound sense of relief. I looked into my heart and thought... this is it. I left my apartment and went to the front door; I looked out and couldn't see her. Was she playing a cruel trick? Was she still in Tahiti? My heart sank. Then I looked down the road, about 100 metres, a taxi had pulled up, and there she was getting out and pulling a wheelie bag behind her. She had stopped at the wrong building! But she was here! The thin, beautiful, vulnerable girl I had met only four weeks ago at 'Tango Night'.

We walked towards each other and our smiles grew larger and larger until we stood opposite each other, just looking into each other's eyes. No hugs, no kisses just a long penetrating stare that seemed to last an eternity. I felt elated, almost dizzy with excitement and expectation.

I wheeled her bag back to my place and at first we made small talk, and then, I couldn't hold back any longer, I had to have her in my arms, close to me. I just hugged her for what seemed to be a moment held in time. I looked down at her face, compelled to kiss her, when I realised I was looking at an ungodly cold sore on her lip!!! Not big, but big enough to stop a kiss cold, then and there. Oh well, they heal I thought and instead we started talking.

We commenced a dialogue that began to really introduce us to each other. She told me piece by piece about herself and her family history. We went to lunch at Watson's Bay and talked about her childhood.

After our sumptuous feast of fish and oysters, we thought a slow romantic walk along the beach was fitting. She began to really relax and open up, telling me about her past relationships, and then finally, she got up to the part involving Marco, I was all ears. I was especially eager to hear why they had broken up.

Apparently, he had met a girl when he had returned home to Italy some three years ago. They were living in Sydney at the time and she suspected something was going on; he would take an increasing amount of calls at odd times of the weeknight and weekends stating it was work. He was constantly sending messages when he thought she wasn't focusing on what he was doing. The quick glances her way before texting were so out of character for him and so obvious to her. He would tilt the phone so she couldn't view the screen; he would pop his head into a room to see if she was there, and then quickly retreat. And his phone was now constantly on silent when he was home. She had deduced that these were the sly activities of a person intent on hiding something from his so called 'loved one'.

This went on for months and finally she and a girlfriend decided to go through his things. They found a love letter that he had received and had hidden among his work papers. She confronted him about it and he confessed. She told me she was devastated. She ran out of the apartment and walked for hours. He had broken her trust and her heart. She felt deceived and lost.

I listened as though this story was a biblical revelation, holding her hand and offering my insights into condemnation and compassion. I couldn't stand the idea that someone had hurt her and I abandoned my emotional neutrality, and from that moment onwards I felt an immense antipathy toward him. She said he had always been cold but this had sealed their fate. He begged forgiveness; after all they had been together for almost seven years. She said he asked for just one more chance, and she caved in and conceded. She also added in his defense, he actually seemed to change for a couple of months.

At this point he had been offered a promotion at work and an opportunity to work in his firm's Singapore office. It was a new start and off they went. She explained that after a couple of months he lapsed back into his workaholic habits. They drifted apart and she became intolerably unhappy and decided to end it once and for all. I knew then at that moment in time that I was in love with her, her vulnerability, her fragility profoundly moved me. I just wanted to protect her and to nurture her, and I wanted to love her completely and unreservedly.

Her hotel was just ten minutes from me, so I dropped her off that evening and went home and slept with the knowledge that we were both moving towards each other emotionally. I didn't have to push, there was no resistance. There was at this stage, only the joy of sharing experiences and making lasting memories together.

21 August

One of the best days of my life,
sleep tight my beautiful Simone
xx
10.31pm

22 August

I cannot begin to express how grateful
I am, for your generosity and your ability to make me feel so beautiful and special.
I had one of the greatest days of my life yesterday.
I cannot believe you are now in my life. I'm blessed.
I have goosebumps as I write these words down.
Fair bet you may be with me for some time to come. hahaha....
Have a wonderful day and night and I look forward to seeing you tomorrow. xoxox Thanks again xoxoxo
6.50am

Over the next few days we went for drives to the country and ate romantic dinners in some of Sydney's finest restaurants. I had also planned a special surprise; a night at the Opera House to see La Bohème. It was, as expected, absolutely fantastic. I'm an avid opera fan. I love the spectacle of the whole thing. The big sets, the elaborate costumes and of course the sound of majestic harmonies the singers magically produce. It was a brilliant performance. It was a brilliant night, an absolute standout and one that I will never forget. For it was this incredible night that we became lovers.

The power of our connection was magnetic, and I felt like I had already made love to her through our deep communication, our long endless stares and our closeness. The step to consummate our

41

extraordinary connection was tender and gentle. We arrived back at my place after the Opera, basking in the incredible few hours we had just experienced. I just had to have all of her. The minute we stepped into my apartment I couldn't wait, I closed the door and started gently kissing her neck, she surrendered into my arms; she was intoxicating. Pushing my body up against hers, she could feel my readiness; I grabbed her hand and gently took her to my bedroom. She dimmed the lights. I wanted to discover her, inhaling every moment and with my tender touch I slowly undressed her. Her silhouette was so delicate, her skin so soft, her scent so arousing. It was so natural, she was alluring, her body ready to be one with mine. It was like nothing I had ever known; unspoken, deep, tender and gentle. We looked into each other's eyes as we held each other, feeling a connection that we both agreed later was extraordinary. I was euphoric and gripped for the first time with a profound sense of wellbeing and happiness. She was the mirror image of my emotional experience.

I would learn later that she had a self-image problem with her body and was rarely comfortable to be naked in the light. This is confusing for a man, because we don't see or view the so-called flaws as imperfections. When we are about to have sex or make love, or however the term fits, we certainly don't start thinking about flat chests, or cellulite, or fat ankles. And for me, right now, in this moment, after spending weeks apart getting to know one another, all I saw was a beautiful, petite, gorgeous woman in front of me; a woman I had come to care for deeply.

When two people connect intimately, there is something to be said for the way that you approach sex. It is intense and fulfilling. There is nothing crass or dirty about it. It takes you both to a higher level of bonding and that's what had happened to us during the course of the night. We had consummated this union so beautifully that there was no doubt in our minds that we were on the journey to coupledom.

The next day we walked to the city to go to the Art Gallery, and down to The Rocks to look at the shops. We went into one of my favourite bookshops and I took her in my arms and we danced to the music playing, oblivious to others looking at us. It was mad, exciting and impulsive. I wanted this moment, this feeling to last forever. However, reality struck and sadly I was reminded we were on a timetable, and the clock was ticking and tomorrow she was leaving. We spent the rest of the day in bed. I laughed that we had made love but never kissed. The cold sore was almost gone but I just couldn't bring myself to kiss her. We laughed but didn't care. Our focus was on making love and due to her upcoming departure; there was now a sense of urgency that was attached to it.

I loved how she wrapped her long slender legs around my waist, our hips fitting perfectly together, her skin was as soft as silk and our eye contact was electric. Whenever we had this physical closeness, I slipped easily inside her; she let out a low groan. I felt her gently quiver as we made love, her rhythm with me as I slowly moved in and out of her was faultless, we were a union of sexual perfection.

As our rhythm grew more intense and frantic, her moans grew louder. I pulled her legs up and around my neck, entwining my fingers in her toes. Our stare into each other's eyes was like a beam of electricity. Nothing or no one could break it. We were the only thing on this earth that existed at that moment in time. I was throbbing and I could feel her hot wetness pulsating around me. We were both on the brink of cumming. We both exploded into a full-bodied orgasm. I felt euphoric as I flowed deeply into her. Afterwards I lay on top of her, hot, sweaty, breathless and completely spent. I could feel the remnants of her orgasm as she lightly shuddered sporadically beneath me, I was still deeply inside of her, she was so tight and I was so hard. We were made for each other. I was convinced of that more than ever now. This was raw, spontaneous passion. I thought of how corrupted our culture had become after years of watching porn and how formulaic sex had been for me up until this moment.

She took her leave that night to catch up with friends. Every time she was away from me, I felt such emptiness. I was like a lost puppy yearning for my mistress's return. It was quite pathetic. I'm a 51-year-old man for God's sake!

25 August

> Thank u for the most beautiful 5 days of my life. U have shown me what love feels like again, and u have stolen my heart...
> Your Michael xoxoxo
> 7.28pm

> Michael words will barely express my true feelings right now. My heart is truly yours and I hope you will take care of it. I am overwhelmed at how I am feeling. My telling you that I love you was a momentous moment. I have uttered those words only once, and never to Marco in my 7 years with him.
> I am so completely in love with you!!!! And this is only the start. I am now so excited about our life when I make the move from Singapore, it scares me to have to even go back, but I know you sensed that. You give me strength to go and face the turmoil that awaits me over there. The universe has spoken and you are my destiny. I will never forget these past few days.
> xoxoxo
> 7.45pm

> My beautiful Simone...
> What a message...
> Well we will make each other
> happy, there is no doubt. My
> unit feels so empty. I have been
> sitting thinking and reliving every
> minute. I love u !!!
> And it already hurts not to have
> u here!!! I am pretty tired, I will
> dream of u!! Good night my
> darling xoxoxo !
> 8.07pm

Yes, I had uttered those three words – actually texted before I realised... "I love you" sent into cyber-space.

Next day I met her for our farewell, we were both upbeat about it, albeit slightly forced on my part. Things weren't that dire, after all, she was coming back in about a month to live in Sydney and she had told me she wanted to be with me. But I still couldn't help but feel like I was losing a part of myself when she wasn't close by.

She had attended a number of job interviews whilst visiting, and had thought they had gone well. So fingers crossed one would come through. I hailed a taxi and as it pulled up I couldn't help noticing the expanse of glorious blue sky, as though the Gods were saluting our love, and to top it off, a sky writer had just drawn a heart!! This had to be a sign. We were meant for each other. She left in the taxi and I walked back home, re-living every moment, every nuance, and every emotion of the last five beautiful days.

26 August

See u soon !! Xxx
11.01am

I love you my darling man!!
Please take care xoxo
11.04am

Unbelievable, one second after u
got in the taxi a monk walked up
to me and gave me a token of
love I love u so much!!!
For us together!! Xxx
11.17am

Can you believe all the signs the
universe keeps sending??
Hilarious!! Xoxo
11:33 am

Song in taxi called "true love"
11.37am

The signwriter in the sky...Big
heart ohhhh just for us Xoxo
11.38am

U can catch it soon!!
BTW we met on the 19 th July, so
6 weeks on Friday!!
Unbelievable.
Miss u so much already!!! Xxx
11.40am

Have a great flight my darling!!
Xxx
11.41am

She hadn't even been gone ten minutes before we were texting again. It was addictive. We couldn't get enough of each other. And with this growing addiction,came the addictive desire and need to be never far from each other's thoughts.

26 August

I cannot tell you how much I miss you after only just saying goodbye!!! I just confided in Troy, my friend from our first encounter at The Crystal, to our wonderful last 5 days.
He is the first person I've told so far, how madly in love with you I am. You must meet him when I get back. He is a very dear friend now.
12.43pm

Would love too!! We should have a party when u get back with all our friends!!! Xoxo
I love u sweet heart and my heart glows!! Xoxoxo
12.48pm

Check out Chanel Mademoiselle perfume Do u know it? If u like it I would like to buy u a bottle, a little present too spoil my Simone a little !!xxx
12.51pm

Yes I know it and I think it's divine.
But, you don't need to buy me anything.
You have spoilt me enough in the last week.
Please respect this, as I don't need your gifts, just your heart.
xoxo
1.13pm

Looks like we will have our first '
fight ' My darling, u have to
understand I have not had
anyone to buy things for for so
long, and it gives me genuine joy
and pleasure to give u presents.
So when u get back I will have a
few little things for u
I love u Xxx
1.18pm

I love you too!!! and I'll say it
again, I don't need your gifts. The
things that I treasure most and
leave the most impression, are
the things we do together that
cost us nothing; walks at sunset,
cooking at home, lying on the
beach side by side, browsing
through book shops, stealing
glances in a crowded
supermarket. I don't need to be
showered with extravagant gifts,
sure they're great to have, but
essentially, they're not the things
that make my heart swell.
1.23pm

I know, I know and those values
are just one of the things I love
about u.
But just occasionally, I might just
want to spoil u But all with
consummate taste ... xoxo
1.25pm

Maybe we can plan another road
trip to that shop in Leura when
I'm back? I might get one or two
special things there to
compliment and upgrade my
future "IKEA" collection. Maybe
we can get some beautiful things
for our future??? Hope that
thought doesn't throw u.

But it's hinting at some of that serious 'shit' that u r going to remind me about to discuss !!
♡♡♡
1.29pm

It is locked in my calendar as a reminder for the 30th September!! lol
1.31pm

Good! But with your punctuality problem we may have to discuss it a bit earlier!! Xxx
1.33pm

Ok, so this is it. I'm on the plane and about to depart.
I will let you know when I have landed safely.
God I miss you so much already....Please don't forget me my darling man. Have a wonderful day, and think of me.
xoxoxo
1.43pm

My darling Simone, when u read this I will probably be asleep. Dreaming about us.
A few thoughts... I watched the sunset tonight without u. It was like a book without words.
I need u to add meaning to my world.
I know that u have quite a bit of work to do to get ready to come back. I am also worried that the reaction at home may be very difficult if u need me I am here for u 24/7. I think u should stay away from Marco for the time being. Can u stay at a hotel tonight and with your friend tomorrow? Please think about it.

I just want you to be safe. The last 5 days will be with us forever...I still can't believe what feelings u have stirred. I am totally in love with u!!!! I want us to have a wonderful future together!! All my love, your Michael. Xoxoxox
8.39pm

I was reminded of what a dear friend, Scotty, had told me once. You know with certainty the best relationships are those where everyday life is intimate, passionate and loving. One big foreplay. Where you both hold one another's look, you brush by one another intentionally touching, you passionately kiss on the sofa just for the sake of it not going to sex necessarily, you bounce through the door from work and lift her up and say "hi", listen to one another with the TV off just talking about anything and nothing; more focused on the sheer thrill to be in each other's space. She sits on your knee to talk, just because she can and runs her fingers through your hair to let you know that right at that moment there is nowhere else she'd rather be, and sex becomes just a beautiful extension of everyday life and is such a statement of an intimate life together and with these thoughts flowing through my mind, I was in no doubt whatsoever I had comfortably and effortlessly arrived together with Simone, to a very blissful destination; the journey ends where lovers meet...

FIVE

27th August - Day 39

Tying - up loose - ends

Once she had returned to Singapore, we settled back into a comfortable rhythm of texting and Skyping.

27 August

> Hey Darling, I have arrived safely and to the most beautiful message from you!!
> Its late and you will be asleep, but I had to respond. You need to know how your words affect me. I am so utterly in love with you.
> I feel like a giddy teenager, experiencing something so powerful and overwhelming.
> I am slightly anxious about the upcoming weeks, but knowing that I have you to come back to is such a beautiful notion, it gives me such strength to get through the next
> 3 weeks. I long for the day when I'm back in your kitchen being your official onion cutter...lol

Exploring deserted beaches at sunset together, showing you my favourite hidden gems around Sydney Harbour, take the soft part out of the bread for you, and make love as many times as is humanly possible in a lifetime. My life seems to make sense now, and I have a purpose….everything has fallen into place and is crystal clear.
I love you…I LOVE YOU !!!!!
I will speak tomorrow at a decent hour. Thanks for your concern, but please don't worry, I can handle myself. I'm a lot tougher than I look xoxox
11.34pm

28 August

I'm having a restless night…can't sleep!!!
The world is such a crazy place right now.
So much unrest and war. Why can't people get along?
I know…a silly naïve concept to a very intricate problem.
I think I'm seeing things in a different light now with so much love in my heart, I guess I expect everyone else to have the same feelings I do right now.
You have restored my faith in humanity and definitely in love. I hope you're having better luck with your sleeping habits. We are a funny pair…very complimentary to one another's foibles. I love you xoxoxo
6.40am

Morning, my darling. I love
calling u my darling.
I slept better last night, but I felt as
though I was definitely fighting off
a cold. I close my eyes with your
vision, and wake
with your vision !!! ♡ I
love u very much I am thinking of
working from home today. I'm really
tired and lonely for u. Can't
wait to see u!! Xoxo
6.45am

She had said it would take about four weeks to wind up her affairs in Singapore. Suddenly it came to me like a bolt of lightning. I suggested that since she had reorganised her world to come to Sydney it was entirely reasonable for me to reorganise my world and visit her in Singapore. The next time we Skyped, I revealed my plan.

28 August

Sweetheart it was so good
talking with you.
I apologise for my emotions,
I feel like I have no control over
them, and I'm aware that I let
them run away with me, but its
only because I'm feeling
overwhelmed with love for you.
and you make me feel so
amazing, it scares me at times.
But know this.....I have utmost
faith in us and even though at
times I'm slightly wary, I have no
doubt about my decision....and
you are a big part of my decision
in moving.
I can't believe you are coming!!!
I'm so happy!!! ♡ ♡ xoxo
11.33am

> My darling Simone I
> understand.
> I love u... Don't worry, just fill
> your heart with love and kisses. I
> had to see u before u came back.
> I ache to be with u !!!! So we will
> do it together ... And I have no
> doubts either
> Xoxoxo
> 12.01pm

So, I set about organising flights and accommodation and thought this was an incredibly exciting chapter in a love story that, for once, was real and tangible.

28 August

> Booked!!!!!!!! So excited xxx
> The future belongs to those who
> believe in the beauty of their
> dreams. I want u to move
> confidently in the direction of
> yours and know that I will be
> right beside u xxx
> 3.30pm

> I've been asked by Immigration
> to prove I have an address in
> Australia, any chance I can use
> yours? lol, it's not a cunning
> plan.... or a hint, although you
> have offered me the world
> already. ;-)))
> 3.38pm

> 17/77-79 New Sth Head Rd
> Double Bay 2027.
> Just finished Henry. What a
> wonderful series. can't believe
> the incredible infidelity of these
> people!! We will watch it from
> start to finish.

How r u feeling?? Xoxoxo
3.43pm

I hope I don't scare you ???
3.49pm

The whole thing scares me a little.
The speed in which we have accelerated is most terrifying.
I'm pretty close to being ready to depart here. Just a few logistical errands to complete and I'm done….hello new life!!!
4.03pm

I like the idea of flying back together and starting a new life together!! Do I scare u???
4.05pm

YEP!!!!!!
4.05pm

Yes I scare u??? Or yes to flying??
4.06pm

A little, but it's all positive xoxo
4.07pm

And fly back??
4.07pm

Do I really scare you????
4.08pm

Yes because you are so committed straight up, and it's all so quick, but I love it at the same time. Just need to work out time it will take for my stuff to get shipped over. God I love you so much!!!!!
4.12pm

I can't begin to describe the euphoria, the excitement, the sense of well-being that had overcome me. I had been catapulted into an entirely different world. I had just booked international air tickets, accommodation and was counting down to the trip to Singapore.

I am heading to bed soon to dream about us.
Talk tomorrow have a great night.
My thoughts and love r with u
Xoxoxo
9.54pm

A few more boxes to fill and a couple of farewells to organize, and its slowly coming together. Remember to take your vitamins...lol...direct orders from Nurse Betty...aka ME!!!!
9.56pm

I just met my friend's husband. They generously offered me so much support in terms of storing my space and accommodation etc...
I feel so blessed. The whole move is happening effortlessly...what's the saying? Smile and the world smiles with you.
Well Sir, Your big grin is causing massive tremors that is making my earth shake in wonderful fits of laughter... can't wait to see you xoxo
10.15pm

29 August

> Morning!! Yes I woke up at 5.30!! Thinking about U!! And yes I agree that our meeting was a life changer. Were so lucky. It's quite intoxicating!!!
> I am drunk with happiness knowing that u r in my life. I know that we r serious people that would not start something frivolous, and after our first 5 days together, I am so confident that it is a perfect fit. And it feels effortless, and yes I care about u, and want to spoil u, within reason!!!! I will send u the dates and if they work, we can leave together. Quite symbolic when u think about it
> And it's not that long
> My darling Simone
> I love u so much!!! I arrive on 12th so it isn't that long. U moved your world to see me, I want to show u, I can move mine to be with u. Are u in bed???
> 5.41am

Wow, wow, wow...Again I wake up to beautiful messages from you. I'm hoping our high speed romance won't hit a side rail and crash with dire consequences.
I love you....Bring on the speeding fines I say!!!
6.13am

> Yes, perhaps, but I want to live the dream with you!!!
> Trust me my darling as I trust u.
> Let's Skype ?? xoxo
> 6.30am

I'm home after 6pm my time. I have a few errands to run after work. Hey, I trust you enough to move my whole life to another country….that's pretty big darling. xoxoxo
6.35am

Perfect!!! My heart is soaring. I will be home about 6pm.
7.07am

Darling, I don't want u to think I am presumptuous but I have reserved a ticket.
I didn't want to miss out if the flight gets booked.
We can of course discuss tonight? Please don't be concerned or cranky with me?!
10.01am

Mine is soaring too ♡
10.04am

What do you mean??? Reserved a ticket for me to come back with you???
10.04am

Yes
10.05am

WHAT???!!!! You are CRAZY! Needs discussion tonight.
10.10am

Ok... Crazy about u!!!! ♡ ♡ ♡
10.11am

Fantastic...I have been a travel agent this evening and our magic is working!!!!
I can't wait till I tell u all the fabulous things on our agenda in

Singapore!! ♡ ♡ ♡
10.12am

Sorry for being the bearer of bad news, but Marco is home so I can't Skype. I feel like I'm rubbing my newly found happiness in his face.
I hope you understand. I can Skype now from my phone without video?
6.10pm

August 30

Sure, shall I ring u??
6.11pm

I always feel on top of the world after we talk.
Good night!!! I love you!!!xoxoxo
9.01pm

Oh my darling I just got massively panicked!!!
All these questions swirl around my mind.
Am I doing the right thing? Are we rushing this?
I know without a doubt I love you.
I just feel overwhelmed....Breathe!!!!
10.41am

Disregard my text, a small freak out. xoxo
10.42am

My darling, I know we r doing the right thing!!!! Don't panic. I love u xxxx
1.11pm

All good. It was a momentary panic attack.
Well it's official. I just had to say'
The Official' oath to a government officer saying my departure is permanent. It is now a reality...and we are doing this....yikes!!! excited and nervous!!
1.30pm

U jump ... I jump. I love u! xx
1.32pm

I can't believe I had uttered those immortal words from Titanic!!!

Hi!! Finished meeting and thinking of u at the same time. Multi skilling!!
I hope u r feeling better Simone, these r big steps to take for both of us. But we like to dance in book shops!!Seriously I would be concerned if u were not a bit anxious. But I am right beside u, and will be every step of the way!! I love u!!!
1.36pm

I feel very supported by you, and because we are both invested, I feel 100% better than I was. It's just nerves, but nothing can stop this train...we are on a mission.
1.49pm

Thank u!!! What a beautiful thought!! Our journey together!!
Don't worry I have no doubts or reservations. Actually I do have a reservation, At the Marina Bay Sands! To see u!
2.15pm

That's so exciting!!! On my way to terminate my Superannuation. I will need to use your address again, so they can post my refund.
2.25pm

Sure!!!! Not a problem. Will we be able to Skype this afternoon?? Xxx
3.01pm

I'll let you know when I'm back!!xoxo
3.02pm

Ok Have fun !!! Xxx
4.00pm

31 August

I told Marco when I will be leaving for Sydney, but I couldn't bring myself to saying I was spending last 5 days in Singapore with you in a beautiful hotel. That would've been hurtful. I HATE lying though. One thing that I can't tolerate is any form of dishonesty.
Promise me that our relationship will thrive on absolute trust, complete honesty and openness. Never should we have any secrets or hide anything from each other. My experiences in the past have proven that without these ingredients, we will not have a future.
11.09am

These r my values and I promise that I will live by them with u. I feel I can trust u with every

61

truth, and I hope u feel the same. All my love Your Michael xxxx P.s it was the right decision xxxx
11.30am

This is so fantastic. Everything is so crystal clear, and the world makes sense.
I love you so much!!! ♡ ♡
8.36pm

Ditto ♡ ♡ ♡
8.38pm

I'm out with friends, but nothing they say is computing with me. I feel like the mute button is switched on. You are the only thing that is registering in my thoughts. You are constantly on my mind. You consume my every being, my cells, my thoughts,
My emotions. I can honestly say...
I've never felt anything close to this before....EVER!!! I hope this doesn't freak you out?!? I just need to express this to you, and feel like you allow me the platform to tell you this.
The trust I have placed in you is enormous, but feels totally normal.
I want to be the best partner to you, and make up for every mistake other partners may have done to you in the past.
I love you Mr Sherman!!! ♡ ♡ ♡
8.57pm

Wow!!!! Your message has made my day. Darling, it doesn't scare me one bit. It's exactly how I feel and I

guess we r both in this now 2
♡ ♡s beating as one. I love u
little Simi. Thank u for opening your
heart. It's a wonderful feeling. We will
make each other very happy!!!
Heading to bed and I will be dreaming
about u
xxx ♡
9.43pm

Have a wonderful night...
I'll be dreaming about you later
9.45pm

1 September

Marco has invited some mutual
friends over,
I had plans, but they JUST
cancelled at the 11th hr, so I
think I'll hang at home. I'm
actually surprised how well we
get on, since I've told him I'm
going. So baby not long now until
we will be together.... ♡ ♡
7.25pm

Well I want u two to be friends.
And I understand how u feel.
But now I have found u!!!!
And my world has changed!
Xoxox
7.35pm

My heart is overflowing with
love!!! ♡ ♡ ♡
7.36pm

Countdown?? 10 days ♡ ♡
7.38pm

4 September

Soooooo it's just become a reality after actually seeing the ticket......wowsa.....I AM SO EXCITED!! butterflies, goosebumps and a BIG grin are just a few of the symptoms my body is displaying... lol.
Have I told you I love you today??? ♡♡♡
12.22am

Hey Michael, so I had a great talk with Marco tonight. I guess that's the thing when you've been with someone for over 6 years, they can read you pretty well, and he knew that I was feeling uncomfortable with something.
So I was able to be honest and tell him about my real departure date. There is nothing I hate more than dishonesty, I told you this before. But as predicted, and the reason for me lying in the first place, he was not very happy. But not my problem anymore. I just can't tell you how relieved I am that everything is transparent.
Tell you more when we speak.
Love you ♡♡♡
10.16pm

5 September

My darling Simone, I understand. My only concern is your well being and safety. It must be very awkward and uncomfortable. I am sorry ♡♡♡
I love u so much. I will be at a

breakfast this morning with clients then back home to pick some stuff up. We may be able to Skype.
And please don't be upset as I am here for u xoxoxo
6.12am

Morning... How's the meeting going?
I'm fine, no need to worry. As I said, I'm SO happy I was able to tell him. Nobody deserves be lied at or treated with dishonesty! There is so much to deal with still, I feel a little run down, but knowing you are the light at the end of my tunnel, is such a fabulous and comforting feeling. see you in a week... lots of love xx
7.13am

Hey, I have a quiet moment and my thoughts turn to u. What u mean to me? U allow me to be uncool. U r like a beam of sunlight that has shone into my world.
U give me joy just thinking about u now and talking to u just a couple of hours ago.
I just want to say, I love u Simone Martinelli ♡
10.12am

I just got all teary reading your message.
You need to understand that my feelings are EXACTLY the same. My anxiousness seems to have disappeared and I feel completely at ease and relaxed. Love is a funny thing. Changes your whole way of thinking. I

love you, I trust you and I can't wait to see you.... ♡ ♡

5.30pm

12 September

Good morning!!!! Well I woke up at 4.39 am!! Just read your message.
I can't wait to hear all your news !!!
Yep it's the 12th !!!! ✈ ✈ ✈ ✈ In a few hours I will be on my way!!! I am so excited, "the journey ends where lovers meet" My darling Simone our journey is about to begin! I love u!!! ♡

4.41am

Good Morning!!!! Yahhhhh...the day has finally arrived. Tonight I will be with you...WOW, I'm super excited ......I'm going out with a friend for lunch. When are you leaving home again? I love you!!! ♡ ♡ ♡ ♡

8.39am

SIX

12th September - Day 55

Destination: Singapore

The long awaited day arrived to take the taxi to the airport, then a short respite in the lounge, and finally the moment of boarding the plane. Travelling at the pointy end of the plane is an entirely different world in itself. You are treated like a king, and I was the new Master of the universe. I was in love and was hurtling towards the woman I knew was ... "The One".

I hadn't been to Singapore for many years. This oriental metropolis had changed so much since my last visit. It is an extraordinary charming city with a thriving pulse.

The flight was wonderful, good movies, food and wine. I think I was the first person off the plane and through customs, I saw my name held on a white board by my allocated driver who collected my small wheelie case. We drove quickly to the Marina Bay Sands hotel. My heart raced, but at the same time I seemed to feel a serenity and peace of mind which I had rarely known.

The car pulled up at the hotel lobby and I got out and looked into the entrance. I saw her sitting, looking up at me; she smiled, stood up and walked towards me. We stopped about a foot from each other and stared into each other's eyes. That seemed to be our thing. Every time we first see each other, we stop, stare and drink in the essence of each other, scrutinizing every cell and detail. We were getting drunk on love.

"Hello, I'm here now" I said, and with that she collapsed into my arms and hugged me with all her strength.

We went up to our room which was located on the 18th floor and just marvelled at the view over Singapore Harbour. It was magical; the lights, the boats and two people standing together with a sense of unity and destiny. I just couldn't wait to undress her. I looked at her and with the beautiful unspoken language of lovers she unbuttoned her shirt. Again, her silhouette took my breath away and as she walked toward me, naked in the dim light, I was already hard, standing speechless and frozen by her beauty. This woman was in command of me body and soul and it felt incredible. She gently undressed me, touching and feeling every part of me and it was mesmerizing. I was intoxicated by her scent and as we kissed deeply, her hands tenderly discovered my readiness to be inside her. I gently bit her lip. I hadn't kissed her passionately in Sydney; I wanted all of her, lips and all. We gently slid onto the bed, and she quietly whispered, "take me" in a soft and shaky voice.

I gently parted her legs and with no words I slipped deeply inside her, our eyes locked, it was as if I had known her all of my life. We kissed as deeply as we made love, shaking and quivering, discovering each other in a way that was different to Sydney, deeper and more profound. Our love had grown and now I could kiss her as deeply as I could make love to her. Her kisses were as moist as her body, sensual and tender. We made love over and over again, my hands and lips discovering every part of her; it was passionate and without reservation until we finally fell into a deep slumber entwined in each other's arms. We woke as we fell asleep, cradling each other; skin to skin.

Over the next four days we planned a number of outings and dinners and walks. We were actually living together and this was not lost on us. The intimacy was intense. It was as if we were on a honeymoon and inevitably our love grew. Our connection grew. Our friendship grew.

On the second day I began to feel a little unwell. The days were still very hot and the humidity extreme. I wasn't used to the climate and the humidity was overwhelming.

That night I went to bed with a fever, and woke in a cold sweat. I slept poorly and knew in the morning I had picked up a virus. I had come all this way to pick up my girl, my future, and to be struck down with illness was just cruel. I was determined to fight this.

Simone went down to the chemist and obtained some cold and flu tablets. She played the perfect nurse, and even though I was in a foreign city, I felt completely at ease, knowing that I had someone with me, who firstly, was a local and knew her way round the city to get to a chemist, and secondly, loved me and would look out for me. I took a couple of the tablets and slept off the symptoms. Thankfully I felt refreshed and better the next morning.

We toured around Singapore visiting the Sunday Artist markets, The National Museum of Singapore; we bought some T-shirts and some other gifts, at the Markets of Artists and Designers, we strolled like gushing teenagers through The Botanical Gardens and we indulged in High Tea at Raffles. She showed me all her favourite places and for the first time she said that she was actually enjoying Singapore. I suggested to her it was most probably because for the first time she was exploring the city as a tourist!

The days flew past and soon we were standing at the airport check-in for our return trip to Sydney. She had discarded her life in Singapore and was coming back to Sydney with me. I was still in a state of semi disbelief. This had occurred so naturally and the string of events leading to this point of departure from Singapore had flowed so easily. I knew it was meant to be. I had never been so completely sure of anything in my whole life. Our love was forming a bond that I thought would be indestructible.

We boarded the plane knowing that we were about to start a life together, a life as partners. A life of inter- dependency. As everyone on the plane prepared for the evening and settled into their extended bunk beds, we sat opposite each other and dined amongst the stars. We spoke very little, and looked into each other's eyes with a gentle softness that was quite exquisite. It was a dinner party I will never forget.

When we landed in Sydney the air was sweet, the sun was shining and such was my happiness I thought angels were singing.

SEVEN

20th September - Day 63

Settling in Sydney town

Simone had arranged to stay with her friend Peta in Manly. Peta was now madly in love with her new man Kurt. I'd only briefly met Kurt but he seemed a perfect gentleman and a real asset to her. I had actually met Peta the first night I met Simone at "Tango Night" and would definitely get to know her over the next few months. She was quite lovely, and I remember thinking had I not have met Simone first that night, I might just have easily engaged in conversation with Peta, and then this book may not have been written. I guess that's fate, eh?

Back in Singapore over dinner one night, I had explained to Simone I wanted her to have a new life and to be independent. After the experience of the last relationship I didn't want her to feel under any obligation to move in with me immediately. I wanted her to have freedom; to choose me; to come to me of her own free will. She said she loved me even more after I'd said these words.

So over the next couple of weeks we went house hunting, looking at various apartments and finally picking a small bed-sitter in Elizabeth Bay. Simone told me that Marco had sent her some suggested locations as they were now getting on quite well since the breakup. I didn't think twice about it at the time

20 September

Hey Darling, few errands today, then off to inspect a flat in Elizabeth Bay.
Want to come with me? I'd love your opinion.
Miss you...!! ♡
2.25pm

Absolutely!!! Is there parking??
Can u send me the address??
Love u!! Xoxo
2.35pm

You're hilarious!! I'm sure somewhere on the street you will find a park, but I don't think there will be a designated park for Michael and his limo...xoxox
It's next door to where I looked on Thursday darling man.
2.38pm

I will meet u there at 4.45. Xoxox
2.43pm

The inspection just got cancelled for the 2nd time today!! That lady is hopeless! So I'll come directly to your place later in the afternoon ok? Xoxo
4.15pm

Simone I Love U ♡ ♡ ♡
4.16pm

And I love you too Michael!!!!
Guess what???
I have 4 inspections on
tomorrow... fear not,
I wont drag you along. There is
one close to you, but WAY above
my price range...lol see you real
soon darling. xoxo
4.38pm

22 September

Application filled out and sent.
Fingers crossed I get it. Then I
can truly feel settled and start
our new adventure. I'm about to
meet friends for a beer at The
Bavarian. Miss you!!!
3.29pm

Hahahaha. Just texted Carly,
thought we might meet her ASAP
to thank her!!
Well that sounds like fun!! Send
me some pics. xoxo
3.30pm

Bummer, don't think the place I
like has built ins.....Looks like I
need to visit IKEA. Want to come
baby? xoxo
3.40pm

Just a few thoughts... It's easy to
say I love u, but to be in love is a
powerfully emotional
experience. Every step I have
taken with u since we met has
just accentuated this feeling.
It's now so apparent that u r part
of my life. I can feel your soul

next to me now, and, forever
xxxxx Yes to furniture shopping
3.43pm

I cannot begin to imagine life
without you anymore. It is not
even a consideration.
I know I got emotional yesterday,
but that's probably because my
love for you is so intense. I love
you Michael!!!
3.56pm

That's wonderful, we r a great
team, we love each other
passionately and we care for each
other I am so happy!! ♡ PS Just
finished Singapore chocolate
4.01pm

So having made the selection she signed the lease and I helped
her move her bags into her new home in Elizabeth Bay. She was just
a 15-minute walk away through Rushcutters Bay. It was perfect.

27 September

Big day for u tomorrow !!!
Little Simi and her first home in
Sydney!!!
Apart from her weekend home
with me!!!
Xoxoxo
6.30pm

Heading home on the ferry.
Packing up...again!!! Last time for
a while.
This is so exciting, still can't
believe how this has progressed
so easily. ♡ ♡
6.34pm

Only just arrived in Manly...
Big cruise ship going out delayed
us. ♡ ♡
7.03pm

Are you ok?? Or simply in bed by
8pm??
I love you and wished to be with
you right now!!!! ♡
8.01pm

28 September

Morning!! Yes I confess I went to
bed early!! Am no good without
sleep. Beautiful day!!! Am going
for a walk. Love u, can't wait to
cook, and blend some fresh juice.
See u about 10.30 ♡ ♡ ♡ xxx
5.56am

Am out for a run!! What a great
day.
Love you!!! xoxo
5.57am

All packed?? Xoxo
7.02am

On my way!! Of course I will be
early!! ♡ ♡
Traffic shocking. They can keep
their north shore!! Xx
10.11am

LOL...Sorry baby!!!
10.16am

Not your fault ... U have seen the
light ♡ ♡ ♡
10.16am

Am here!!!! ♡ ♡ ♡
10.27am

Give me one minute
sweetheart
10.28am

She had signed a six months tenancy, which in both our minds would give her enough time to confirm the decision and my invitation to move in with me. As previously mentioned, we had had a serious discussion in Singapore, deciding that if we still felt the same way as we did now, Simone would move into my apartment, and we would live as a committed couple. In any event her apartment was only a short walk from mine and I had no concerns or reservations that ultimately she would choose to be with me.

30 September

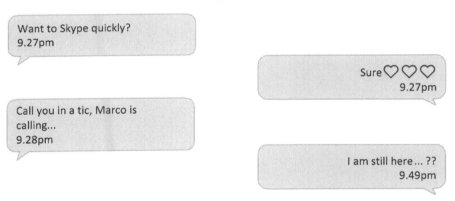

Want to Skype quickly?
9.27pm

Sure ♡ ♡ ♡
9.27pm

Call you in a tic, Marco is calling...
9.28pm

I am still here... ??
9.49pm

I waited and waited for her return text, but it never came. I tried calling her but her line was engaged. What could they possibly have to talk about that would take so long? I had a sense of unease... almost... yes... Jealousy.

I am going to bed...talk tomorrow
10.15pm

Just called, no answer, sleep well and I will see you tomorrow!!!
xoxo ♡
10.15pm

Sweetheart just letting you know Marco called to let me know about a cheap internet connection for me... guess he still feels like he needs to help out. I thought it was really nice of him and very generous. Love you!
Can't wait to see you tomorrow....
10.22pm

Can't sleep. I just know when you're upset with me, and it kills me to think I've caused you any kind of hurt. Please understand that I didn't want to be rude to him when he was doing something considerate towards me. I want to forge a decent friendship with him. Our families are friends and he has been in my life for a long time....and besides that, he is bloody good with technical things. you have nothing to worry about with him and I.
NOTHING!!!!! I'm not sure how I can prove to you that I don't have any romantic feelings whatsoever for him anymore....I can only hope that you trust me and know that I'm deeply in love with you. I wish I could tell you in person and not through such an impersonal way.
Again....I'm so very sorry. xoxox
11.35pm

1 October

> Good morning, I love u so much!!
> Xoxox
> 5.27am

Not my day...forgot handbag at bus stop, had to run back and then I was late at work for training! You know how much it hurts to be late!! Now training basically all day... Are you still mad at me????
8.13am

> How could I be mad with u!!!!
> U r my beautiful girl!!! ♡ ♡ ♡ I was a little annoyed last night, but that was yesterday!! We can discuss tonight. Don't worry
> 8.49am

So relieved to hear!!!! I love you so much!!!
Let's talk tonight?!
9.01am

> This was a little issue, please don't worry about it.
> We will have a lovely dinner and tell each other how much we mean to each other, and then make love !!
> ♡ ♡ ♡ deal??
> 9.05am

YOU'RE ON!!!! ♡
9.10am

Over the next few months we continued to be intoxicated with each other. She would spend weekends with me and sometimes one night during the week. She had secured a great position working for a telecommunications company in the city. Her language skills enabled her to assist at an executive level with the translation of foreign documents. She loved her work, her new colleagues and seemed so happy and told me repeatedly that she loved me and this was the life of which she had always dreamt.

2 October

> I feel so close to u right now ♡ ♡ ♡ ♡ your Michael xx
> 8.31am

Yet again an amazing night spent with you. I am seriously in such a good place right now...so happily in love ♡ ♡
8.48am

> Well date night was amazing!!!
> U bring me joy beyond words.
> Our intimacy is breathtaking. I just want to kiss u and wear your lipstick!!
> I love u and need u!!! It's so beautiful to hold u and touch u. I too am speechless!!! ♡ ♡ ♡
> 9.43pm

It was fabulous. Thank You!!!!
9.49pm

3 October

On a Wednesday night in October she invited me to a function. It also coincided when Australia was playing host to all of the world's naval fleets. The Italian Grand Admiral was the guest of honour. As I walked in, I was met by a very tall blonde lady, who ushered me directly into the VIP area. It was a case of mistaken identity, as Simone was waiting for me in another area. I was handed a drink and immediately introduced to The Grand Admiral. He told me he was without a boat in Sydney after I enquired which one was his... I made a joke that he wasn't much of an Admiral if he didn't have a boat. Definitely a Woody Allan-esque moment but thankfully, he saw the humor and we shared a laugh, but not before there was a long and very awkward silence. I thought it hilarious that I was possibly the only non-Italian at the party, yet here I was hobnobbing with the guest of honour. No doubt they reviewed their security or lack thereof after that little dalliance. I took my leave from the VIP area and went in search of my gorgeous girlfriend.

We had a wonderful evening. Simone introduced me to more of her friends and they were very open and accepting of her much older boyfriend. We danced the night away and by 1.00am I was exhausted, so called it a night and left Simone to enjoy herself with her friends.

4 October

> U looked so beautiful tonight!!! I love u so much. I'm almost home. Sleep well. ♡ ♡ ♡ ♡ ♡
> 1.10am

I'm so glad you got to meet some of the people in my life. You fit right in, and that means a lot to me. you are such a major part of my life. ♡ ♡ ♡
1.32am

> Don't worry u have me, body and soul ♡ ♡ ♡ ♡
> 1.43am

It's late and I feel so alive. I'm going to utilize my time and unpack....
You have my body and soul, but you knew that already no doubt.
Sweet dreams, sweet man!!
2.25am

7 October

> I love u so much!! I love everything about u.
> I hunger for u, I love watching for u, I miss u when u go for a second
> ♡ ♡ ♡ ♡ ♡ ♡ ♡
> 12.51pm

Pinch me!! Each weekend gets better. I love you truly, madly, deeply...Thank u!!
♡ ♡ ♡ ♡ ♡
1.35pm

> This is the most amazing feeling. It blows me away. You make me so incredibly happy!! Thank you! I love you so very much!!! Spoke to my parents.
> Can we Skype? ♡ ♡ ♡
> 2.22pm

Sure thing... I'm just getting dressed.
2.40pm

> Give me 10 ♡ ♡ ♡
> 2.41pm

Okey Dokey
2.41pm

J.D. WATT

EIGHT

8th October - Day 81

Meet the Family

It was time for me now to bring her completely into my life. I told her that I wanted her to meet my parents and my Sydney family. She didn't quite understand the significance of the latter until I explained that I wanted her to meet my ex-wife Miriam and of course my daughter Naomie. I said I didn't need to obtain their blessing, that was not the aim of the exercise, but since our divorce, my ex-wife had become a wonderful friend, and we had supported each other throughout our lives and had created a wonderful daughter.

If Simone was to become a fixture in my new life then there was no reason why she shouldn't meet these people. She agreed but told me that she was possibly more nervous at the prospect of meeting my ex and my daughter than my parents. I said I completely understood but promised that once she had met Miriam, she would instantly understand why I wanted these two women to meet.

For me it was an emotional bridge that I wanted to cross. It was an important steppingstone from my past into my future. My ex-wife and I have an unusually strong bond and we remain prominent in each other's lives, not just because of our daughter. Perhaps it was selfish of me and even unrealistic, but it was very important to me that they could possibly forge a friendship of sorts. Thankfully Simone agreed albeit somewhat with hesitance.

So, for now, I decided to focus more on my parents, and went ahead and booked tickets to fly us to Queensland to meet my parents.

8 October

> Am booking tickets!!
> Are u still there??
> 6.46pm

> Yes sorry....very busy here.
> I need to cancel tonight, doesn't
> look like I'll be getting out of
> here before 8pm and I'm tired.
> What's possibility of booking
> flexible ticket in case I'm stuck
> with work commitments?
> ...actually forget that just book it.
> I'm in. Think I'm scared about
> meeting your folks.
> 7.03pm

> Flight out is at 5.10 pm.
> That should be ok I hope. Only
> one I could get. ♡ ♡ ♡
> 7.05pm

> Great
> 7.05pm

I have been working hard. All booked, flights accommodation, and restaurant on Sat night!! Surprise on Sat night. ♡
7.15pm

Good work...I'm honored you want me to meet your parents, especially so quickly after we've met... still here at work. I'm soooooo tired.
7:39 pm

13 October

Just reflecting on what a wonderful weekend we have had. Great friendship, fantastic sex, cooking, swimming, shopping etc. Some real couple stuff!' Two people who love each other and respect each other.
Well done Simone and Michael!!! Happy Anniversary!!! ♡ ♡ ♡ ♡
I love u!!!
6.48pm

We are so right together. You were the missing piece of my puzzle.
You complete me and make me the best person I can be in every sense...or try to be... I know I want to experiment more with you sexually. I'm a little inexperienced in that department lol..
I love you more than I've ever loved anyone in my life before. We are a great team and I believe we are perfect together.
I LOVE YOU!!!!
6.55pm

> Thank u, I am humbled by your words.
> Let's keep the magic going !!!!
> Xoxox
> 6.57pm

Yes, we had just reached our three-month anniversary, and I was more enamored with her as each day passed. Our professed texts of love were flowing thick and fast. She was like a drug to me, and I needed to see her more than ever. I didn't want to scare her, but in truth, I was ready for her to move in now, but Simone was fiercely independent, and at times very unreliable.

15 October

> I'll check what times the ferry departs.
> I'm swamped here... Not sure when I will get out, but I can't wait to see you. Love date night.
> 5.24pm

> Hi, Again I'm under the pump here. I'm going to bail on tonight. I'm so tired. It will be late when I eventually finish.
> I'm so sorry, I just can't wait to get home and do nothing but sleep.xoxo
> 5.31pm

> Ok, don't worry.
> Go home and rest ...
> 5.32pm

> Finished earlier than expected. heading home now. What a long day.
> I apologise again.
> 6.47pm

Just had a bath... Without u ...
Sad and annoyed. So I am going
to bed soon.
Tomorrow is a new day.
6.55pm

I'm so, so sorry
6.56pm

So am I. U should not build
expectations and then not
deliver. I really miss u. I thought
we had a date. The
disappointment is really hard to
describe! So let's leave it....
7.05pm

Pick up the phone!!!!
SERIOUSLY!!!!
I'm tired. I wouldn't have been
good company... It's not a big
deal, or I thought it wasn't. I
didn't act this way when you
cancelled on me last week. come
on...really???
7.17pm

That's because I got called away
400 miles. I am sorry. Not over
reacting, just miss u terribly. I
don't want to upset u.
I'm going to bed. I love u. Talk
tomorrow. X
7.53pm

I wanted to talk to you not have
an argument via text.
This is crazy...good night.
I'm not playing!!!
7.57pm

Thank u, sleep well. I am very
emotional, don't know why ...
Sorry. X
7.58pm

> I'm actually pissed off now, if
> you want to communicate with
> me then CALL ME... don't text.
> 8.03pm

I called her and we talked for about half an hour, my frustration diffused and we said goodnight. Saturday the 19th would be a work colleague's wedding and I had invited Simone.

19 October

> What a glorious day!!!!
> Perfect day to get married...lol...
> or at least go to a wedding.
> I'm going to stay put here in the
> sun for a while darling, and take
> in the views and the rays. I think I
> may have to go dress shopping
> before the wedding, as I don't
> really have anything appropriate.
> So what time shall we meet??
> And where?? Xoxo
> Should we be expecting to dine
> on chicken feet today?
> 10.03am

One of my lawyers, Lee, a Korean boy was getting married and they had invited us as a couple to the wedding.

> I think I'm having another panic
> attack.
> I realize when I'm on my own, I
> need my own space. I never
> really processed my split from
> Marco before we submerged
> ourselves in our own adventure.
> I don't think I'm where you're
> at... I know I love you, but every
> now and then I need breathing
> space. I needed to tell you this

just now as it's been a constant thought lately.
But know that I love you.
10.33am

I completely understand,
And love u
♡♡♡
10.41am

I didn't understand at all...and this text created a great sense of unease within me.

R u feeling better?? I had my emotional day last Monday. I know how u feel, and we can talk about it. Just thinking there is a nice homes shop near u, we went in there, remember ? They will have a nice gift Saves time. I love u! Need u and am so hungry for u ♡♡♡♡
11.35am

So much better, thank you for asking. Shop sounds great.
11.38am

NINE

21st October - Day 94

The Ex

Slowly things started to change...

Our once easy ride of effortless communication was starting to become a rollercoaster ride of emotions. A pattern was emerging where Simone would switch from one day being a loving and doting girlfriend, to the next day being completely distant from me and announcing she needed to "be alone". This would inevitably occur when Marco would tell her he would be visiting the country. I was perplexed. She had told me he knew about me, that he was happy for her and that he himself had moved on with another girlfriend. Yet every time he arrived in the country, Simone shut down from me and became a recluse.

21 October

> How r u?? Xoxox
> 7.17pm

> Still out. Finished dinner?
> 7.28pm

All finished!! So do I get to see my beautiful girlfriend??? come here?? I will drop u home?? No agenda, I just want to make love to u ♡
7.33pm

I'm going to take a rain check, I'm afraid.
It's getting late; I'm not in the mood for being intimate. Marco arrives tomorrow and for some reason I'm on edge.
8.07pm

Can u call when u leave? Xoxo
8.07pm

I'll call when I get home ♡ ♡
8.08pm

Can u call on the phone when u leave the bar??
8.08pm

Michael, I will call you when I get home.
You are so transparent in your actions.
I'm not in the mood for sex. I told you so already.
8.10pm

Ok, leave it. I am not trying to push, I understand what is happening.
Get an early night. Xxx
8.11pm

Thank you...x
8.13pm

Can't sleep. I know, yet again, I have disappointed you. I have to sort something out that satisfies us both.

I need my own time and space designated just for me, where I don't have to think about anyone else. It sounds so awfully selfish, I know, but I need to find myself, before I can give myself again...Does this make sense to you?

I'm not sure how else I can make it clearer.

I also don't want to be a constant disappointment to you, or forever hurting you with my decisions.

Truth is you scare me. I feel so loved by you, and know how much I love you, that it makes me so vulnerable, it scares me. The whole thing is so amazing, yet, it seems unreal. I don't think you are on the right track to become the love of my life, I think you already are. Nothing in my life has ever been this good, so why now? why has this amazing man chosen me to love? you must think I'm crazy??!! Let's talk when we see each other? please be patient... I'm just trying to work it all out.

♡ 11.30pm

22 October

Good morning ... Quite a message..... I can tell there is something that u need to work through .. Thank u for sharing this. One sentence though, I couldn't understand. ..U said I was not on the right track? Was this a typo? Anyhow, I will give u as much time as u need ... I love u 2 xxxx 8.30am

I meant that you are not on the track to become the love of my life anymore, you are already there...sorry for the long late message.
I just wanted you to wake up with a little more clearer understanding of what was going on in my head. I have to stop feeling like I'm disappointing you if I change my mind about seeing you for a night.
Let me explain in person when I see you next.
I love you so very much! I hope we are still a team??
8.40am

Of course, I want u 2 be happy, but I also want u to be ready in your own time. U don't disappoint me by the way, I can tell u have things on your mind. Remember I can read your mind!! Xoxo 8.45am

Running into meeting.
I LOVE YOU ♡ ♡ let's talk later. 8.55am

22 October

Hey! I'm still working.
How are you? love you!!
5.45pm

94

WE have been full on. Not either of us alone, but together, and that's not a bad thing.
BUT I NEED time alone, every now and then. I'm not saying goodbye, just want some Simone time. See?
I'm disappointing you AGAIN!!! This is not lost on me.
Don't feel low. We are in love. I feel wonderful.
We saw each other over the weekend, and for coffee yesterday, please don't make me feel guilty for wanting to do other things tonight.
6.03pm

Hi, My day was reasonably busy, but I felt sad and uncomfortable all day due to your long text. I have to be honest, it's made me think. What do u need? More time? More space? I know u and I have been full on. And tonight u r busy!! I am Feeling a Little low.
5.56pm

I'm heading home. Have a good night!!
6.30pm

I'm going to bed. I hope you sleep well.
I love you!!! I feel like I'm begging for forgiveness...
9.30pm

23 October

> Good morning...can't wait to see you at 1pm! ♡
> 6.30am

> Good morning!! Hope u slept well too
> Hope u r feeling better today?
> Xxx
> 6.35am

> Feeling good thanks. Talked to Marco about you/us. made me feel great, and him not so good...lol more because he knows what he lost, and he knows, I am lost to him now. We will never be a couple again. So yes, feeling much better. xoxoxox
> 7.08am

> Well I am very interested in your discussion.
> I need to talk to u!! Xoxo
> 7.09am

> Can't wait to see you! xoxo
> 7.30am

> I have a table for us. I am eating first.
> Am starving ... See u soon xoxo
> 7.00pm

4 November

> Hi sweety, what are the dates u r working over Xmas ?? Xxx
> 11.57am

Not working, office will be closed.
However, I think I'm going to shoot home for Christmas to be with my mum. First one alone for her.
I need to be with her.
11.59am

5 November

In case you've gathered I'm a little distant again? I'm just letting you know that MARCO will be in the country. He is just meant to be in Qld, but he has turned up unannounced a few times now, and I wouldn't put it past him…. anyway….just thought I'd share. xoxoxo
11.25am

> Sorry to hear, r u free for coffee now?x
> 12.03pm

> I knew it, u have been on planet Simone again. I can sense it!!!!
> 11.31am

> Can I call ?? Xxx
> 4.56pm

I called her and straight away I could sense her distance. She was very abrupt and short with her answers. I wanted to take her mind off her 'ex' and suggested a holiday together over Christmas. It was brushed over. I persevered and talked about the endless possibilities of our glorious future. I was trying to seduce her with the unlimited romantic possibilities of a Christmas getaway, but my efforts seemed futile. I was doing all the talking and her responses were little more than monosyllabic. She was well and truly disconnected. My thoughts turned to her previous text about Marco being in the country. Whether he was aware or not, and whether it was his intention, he still had an emotional hold over her. It was starting to grate on me.

As patient and understanding as I'd been in the past over this issue, I seriously didn't understand why she was so affected by his presence. It made no sense to me. I could feel myself getting frustrated, so I took my leave from the phone call and bid her goodnight.

5 November

I feel so pressured by you right now.
I love you more than I've ever loved anyone else, but I feel like I'm drowning. Let's talk face to face. This is too meaningful to be diminished by text messages.
10.02pm

I don't mean to, I really don't want to. I love u and u have told me how much u love me. That actually makes me want to do things with u. Is it my parents? Is it to plan a trip overseas? I don't understand! We have to talk. I am so upset. R u home?
10.13pm

It's all good. Don't be upset. We will work everything out, so all our needs are met.
I'm still out with Natalie.
10.19pm

Ok have a lovely night. Xxx
10.20pm

If you're up still, can I come over?
10.23pm

Sure!
10.25pm

Waiting for a cab..
10.33pm

Ok see you soon
10.34pm

6 November

I love u very much.xxx
7.51am

And you know my response to that too xoxo
7.55am

11 November

We need to talk. I have to go home at Xmas. xoxo
8.01am

Sure, we can talk about anything. U can always trust me. I hope things r ok at home ?? Xoxox
8.20am

Not really. My mum is like me and finds it hard to express herself. runs in the family...xoxo
11.30am

15 November

> I apologise for how I came across on the phone.
> Things are running through my head, and I'm not sure how to deal with everything at the moment.
> Anyway, I've booked flights and I

> feel much better.
> I'm so far away from her, I feel she really needs me atm. God I love you so much, I can't tell you what it means to me having you by my side, supporting me.
> 12.14am

I felt quite disappointed that she had just gone ahead and booked a flight home. I still thought she would ask me to come with her, especially after I had suggested a holiday together a few short hours ago, but the request never materialised.

16 November

> Morning!! Hope u slept well!!I love u too!! U have to understand that if we r a team we have to understand each other's moods and support each other!!!
> Don't worry, if u r not feeling happy u have to tell me!!
> Can't wait to hold u in my arms and kiss u !!! ♡ ♡ ♡
> 7.00am

TEN

18th November - Day 122

Meet the Shermans

18 November

> Caught early ferry, r u free for a coffee??
> Spoke to my parents. Such a funny discussion!!
> They r really looking forward to the weekend.
> How should u address them???
> Hahahahah !!
> 7.26am

> How about mum and dad? lol I'm far too formal for that. Mr and Mrs Sherman is far more appropriate.
> 7.36am

> Xxx hahaha!!!!
> 7.40am

> You must still be dining with your daughter.
> Can't wait to see you at the airport.
> What an exciting weekend we

have planned.
Can't wait to meet the in-
laws...haha
A little nervous at the same time.
xoxo
9.40pm

20 November

Good morning miss S, I can't wait for u to meet Naomi, she needs strong elegant women in her life and u represent these qualities!!!
Xox
6.30am

Wow....big responsibility. I'm honoured you think of me like that. I hope she likes me. See you at 5.30 for dinner.
6.50am

We met after work that night and had dinner at one of our favorite restaurants in Potts Point. Whenever we were together things between us were fine. Her anxieties would disappear, and our discussions were light and flowed easily. After I paid the bill, I offered to walk her home, but for some strange reason she was adamant about not wanting me to walk her home. I thought this very strange at the time, as I'd not witnessed such a strong, determined statement of refusal from her. I left her at the end of her street. I walked home reviewing the evening in my mind, wondering at what point I might've said or done something that catapulted her into the need to seek isolation. By the time I got home she had called to explain that Marco had sent some of his clothes to her apartment for her to "store".

21 November

> Morning!!! Thanks for telling me about that issue last night, u were acting a bit strange when we said goodbye!! I love u and u can always talk to me about anything!! I am really looking forward to being with u this weekend.
> Can't wait to hold u in my arms!!
> Xoxoxox
> 6.08am

Morning. I'm super excited, and again I apologise for last night, but I wasn't sure about your reaction to you seeing Marcos stuff in my apartment.
love you!!!
6.15am

I was infuriated to think that he was using her to store his clothes from Singapore. It disappointed me that she seemed to be so weak in matters concerning him. But I said nothing. We had a very important weekend coming up where she was meeting my parents, and I consoled myself that she was making the effort to meet them, and she wouldn't be doing that if he was still a contender.

22 November

> Morning!!! Can u believe the weather??
> Well we r here!! Friday at last!!
> Yay!!
> I love u!!! Xoxox
> 6.14am

I love you too!! I'm all packed and ready to go!!! xoxo
6.30am

I'm getting a lift with my boss to the airport, he was heading to a meeting in that vicinity....couldn't come up with a reason not to accept....didn't think appropriate to tell him about our weekend. Sorry!! I'll meet you there.
12.33pm

That's fine. I will meet u at domestic. Don't tell him. Xxx
12.50pm

love you!!!xoxo
12.51pm

I love u more!!
12.53pm

And we were off to the Gold Coast to introduce my future wife to my parents. Even though I hadn't officially proposed, I had pre-proposed with a beautiful "friendship" ring. I guess I was testing the waters to see what Simone's reaction was, to ensure we were on the same page at still a very early stage in our relationship.

When we were with my parents there was a slightly different dynamic. They were old and becoming frail and they lived in Queensland. Simone said she felt honoured to be invited to meet with them. It was a very big step she said for her and she felt humbled to be part of my new family. My parents were now at the age when travel was becoming a real burden. However once they were aware of the purpose of the visit they seemed to be energised and made a real effort to engage with us socially. We met them at my mother's permanent second home, the Gold Coast casino and she introduced Simone to an Australian institution, the poker machine.

Whilst the Queen mother and the Princess played the machines I sat and talked to my father. I had never had a wonderful relationship with him when I was young. Like any child I instinctively craved the approval of the parent and in this regard I was bringing to my parents the girl I had chosen to be my partner.
"She is very skinny", he said. "Doesn't she eat?"

I said that she seemed only to eat very small meals and was very conscious of her weight.

"You need to feed her", and he looked at me and smiled. "With a couple of more pounds I might like her very much" he said.

And for one of the few times in my life I actually felt close to my father. By that time the girls had returned beaming as they had won a jackpot.

We all left to have lunch and the discussion was relaxed and wide ranging. My father showed a side of his character that I had honestly never seen. He could be charming; he could even attempt humour! Retirement obviously suited him very well. At the end of the lunch we said our goodbyes and took some photos.

My mother commented to Simone "You make Michael very happy", and her reply, "Michael makes me very happy too!"
We went back to the hotel via the cocktail lounge and decided to have a drink, despite the outwardly pleasant behavior of everyone we both felt we had been put under the microscope and examined. Before long we were taste testing our third cocktail. We were so relaxed and comfortable. We went back to our room and I felt closer to her than ever. She had now met my parents and I could see my future wife standing right before me. We couldn't wait to enjoy each other, for the rest of the night. There is something special about

being in a hotel with the woman you love. She was so sexy and when she started to undress in the darkness I knew the night ahead would be raw and passionate. She came over to me in her satin negligee and stood by the bed. As I lay there I slipped my hand between her thighs and felt her wetness, she smiled as I pulled her close throwing her on the bed. I pulled her negligee over her head as she laughed in excitement. I enjoyed her body and she enjoyed mine. We fell asleep entwined in love, the scent of our passionate night filling the room.

We flew back to Sydney, once again enjoying the sense of achievement of being a couple and creating memories that would last forever.

25 November

> What an amazing weekend, I
> love u so Much!!
> U have touched my heart!!
> Xoxoxo
> 7.16am

> Agreed. You have introduced me
> to a whole new world full of so
> many possibilities. I love you. I
> love your family
> You make me happier than I ever
> thought
> I could be!!! Thank You.. .xoxoxo
> 8.13am

ELEVEN

26th November - Day 138

Stepping Up

Yet again we had both managed to step up to the next level of our relationship. When we were together, we were magic. We got on amazingly. That's why I hated when I knew she would go back to her flat, because her moods swings would appear out of no-where. When she was a constant by my side, life was easy. She was happy. I'm no expert, but her mood swings didn't make any sense to me. I wished that they did. Then at least there would be an explanation.

26th November

I love u!!!!!
10.05pm

U r the most beautiful thing in
my life!! Xoxoxox
10.07pm

You are a patient man Michael.
I feel that any man would have

abandoned me because of my mood swings. I know in my heart, you are the one for me. I see us growing old together, and for that, I am eternally grateful. I am yours, and I hope you feel the same way.
I have never been surer of anything more in my life. xoxox
10.15pm

Thank u, u mean the world to me. Don't worry about the mood swings, I am here for u no matter what life throws at u, I love u completely. I have made my decision too!!X
10.21pm

Sleep tight! Counting the hours until Friday night...
10.22pm

Same to u, can't wait to make love to u!
10.23pm

Me too!!! xoxo
10.24pm

The last hurdle in my mind was to now introduce Simone to Miriam and Naomi; the two most important women in my life.

28th November

Hi, hope u had a great day!! Am having dinner with Miriam and Naomi, I told Miriam all about u and she thinks u sound lovely!!!
Xoxoxox
5.41pm

Ohhh man, that scares the bejesus out of me...
Talk later! I love you!!!! ♡ ♡
5.45pm

What time can u leave the office??
The weather is going to be miserable!!!
So fallback position is...
Snack with me and a drink with Miriam and Naomi perhaps later? What do u think?? I love u!! Xxxx
5.50pm

May I say my friend has informed me that meeting the ex-wife is NOT a good idea
5.51pm

Ordinarily I would agree, but this is a very special situation R u comfortable??? I love u and would not do anything to hurt u or damage our beautiful relationship. Xxxx
5.54pm

I'm not sure!!! I think I can handle it.
5.55pm

I am thinking its great curry weather!!!
Apparently Naomi is very excited to meet u!! ♡
5.59pm

Honestly, if it was happening in 5 minutes, I would probably say no!!!! but I'm sure I'll be fine later tonight. Think I'll have a wine or two beforehand.
6.03pm

Well don't worry we will pass and do it another time. Or did u mean the curry??
6.05pm

No let's do tonight. I'm a big girl. I'm sure it will be fine.
6.06pm

Ok let's see, but please understand my focus is u and your happiness and our future!!
Xxx
6.07pm

Thank you! You are so divine. I can face anything and anyone with you by my side.
6.15pm

Leaving the office now. How r u feeling?? Re meeting or dinner??
6.30pm

I'm running a little behind. I'll see you there at 7.30pm x
6.33pm

Ok, I will meet u at Double Bay. Limoncello in Bay Street. The food is fantastic! My friends Giselle and Daniela will look after us! xoxoxoxo
6.38pm

Miriam is unwell ... So no intro
7.02pm

WHAT??? You're not just saying that because I was freaking out????
I seriously don't mind baby.
7.04pm

No she is really unwell :((so it's just u and me xxxx
7.05pm

What a shame, I've just had 3 wines and felt invincible….lol…only joking. Let's still meet at the restaurant??? Same time???
7.10pm

Ok I will meet u there at 7.30 xoxoxo
7.11pm

Damn it, I've missed the ferry and next bus not till 7.16. Sorry!!!
7.12pm

Get a cab I will pay
7.12pm

That's silly. Happy to catch public transport. Not going to be too late.
7.14pm

No problems, would u prefer Indian or Italian … Honestly!??
7.15pm

Surely you know me by now… I'm opting for salad or veggies wherever we end up, so you choose.
♡♡
7.16pm

I finally re-arranged the introduction for a Sunday morning breakfast in Double Bay. Miriam arrived and greeted Simone graciously, and knowing her as I do, I knew she was being sincere.

We all sat down ordered food and chatted. When Simone excused herself to go to the bathroom, I looked at Miriam with expectation and anticipation.

"I like her, she seems lovely." I was so relieved to hear this, although I wouldn't have admitted it to myself, but I knew that if Miriam had reservations it would seriously affect my judgement.

"She doesn't eat, is she anorexic?" she added quickly with some concern.

"I don't know." I replied. I wanted to discuss this further, but Simone was returning to the table.

We drove Miriam to the old house to drop her off and fortuitously Naomi, my daughter was just leaving as we arrived. I was able to introduce Simone to Naomi on the same day. It was a very successful meeting with everyone getting on like old friends. The relief was immense......for everyone.

30   November

I love you so much!!! Can't wait to make a home with you.....
4.07pm

I love u!!
8.15pm

So many amazing things to be grateful for. Our weekend to the Blue Mountains, meeting your family, our amazing moments we spend together, doing simple things. I am so blessed. I love you!
I seriously love you Michael Sherman!!!!

Please don't ever leave me!!!
8.27pm

112

Thank u. I am humbled and
blessed to have u in my life!!
I love u very much...Xxx
8.30pm

TWELVE

6th December - Day 140

Happy 5th Month Anniversary

6 December

> Happy anniversary my darling 5 months! We will open bubbles at home tonight!!! Xoxoxo
> 5.11pm

> And to you too darling!!!
> I can't believe how time has flown.
> Feels like just yesterday I met you.
> Can't wait to celebrate with you tonight!!
> 5.14pm

I began to relax safe in the knowledge that my choice of partner had been validated. I was proud to be with her. She was beautiful, albeit skinny. She was intelligent, refined and funny. She possessed that European elegance I had always admired.

However, as the weeks and months had rolled past from our first encounter, I noticed with regularity, that Simone tended to drink heavily and ate very little. I commented continually and urged her to change her diet. However, she made very little effort to accommodate my suggestions and invariably we would end up at a restaurant drinking, always drinking.

I also noticed that she seemed to receive an inordinate number of phone calls from her ex. Her phone would ring and I would see his name flash across the screen. Sometimes she would excuse herself and take the call. Sometimes she would open and check e-mails and out of the corner of my eye I would see line after line of messages from him.

The constant interruption of his phone calls came to a head one evening when we were at a bar with friends of mine. We were standing together and her phone rang. She pulled it out of her bag and I saw his name.

"I have to take this" She said apologetically and promptly turned and walked quickly out of the room. I thought to myself this was unacceptable behaviour and was crossing the line. One of my friends who was present, also commented that it didn't seem appropriate that she should leave the group to take a call from her ex. Was I jealous? Yes absolutely.

She came back to the group after a few minutes but could see from the expression on my face that I was far from impressed. My whole demeanour changed and she knew the reason why. I said I had to leave, and turned to the group and excused myself; she followed me downstairs and out of the bar onto the street. I think this was our first real fight. Not raised voices but just such profound disappointment.

"This isn't the first time this has happened' I blurted. I told her that I had noticed she was continually taking his calls and it just seemed a little extreme.

"But tonight" I said, "You crossed the line when your phone rang. You jump to attention and ran out of the room. What is going on?"

She suggested that perhaps I was overreacting. I said, "You think about it as I overreact and exit stage left."

I walked away and hailed a taxi. Part of me agreed with her. Perhaps it was a slight over reaction on my behalf, but I had endured this for five months now and over the last month it had increased with intensity to a point where I could actually begin to feel the burden of the third wheel. Something about it raised red flags but I couldn't put my finger on it. I knew what it was like to have a strong bond with an ex. My ex-wife is one of my closest and dearest friends, but I don't drop everything the moment she calls; more out of respect for whoever might be in my company. I certainly don't take every call.

The whole way home I pondered why was she in such close contact with the ex-boyfriend? Was she over him? Was she still seeing him? I soon received a text from her apologising and asking if she could come over and she would explain everything. Ofcourse I agreed and she arrived in a good mood, but reeking of alcohol, and was again able to disarm me of my concerns.

I wanted her in every way. She pulled me close knowing that I just couldn't resist her. She dimmed the lights and undressed. I could never tire of her innocence and our tenderness. It was like nothing I had ever known. Tonight, was no exception; our passion was electric and our movements rhythmic, and on this night, she was more willing than ever. As she held me and guided me insider her, she was wet and so ready, she wanted me and I could feel her captivating me with every quiver and quiet groan as we made love. We came together and both let out a deep euphoric sigh, our skin moistened and bonded by our lovemaking. I wanted to stay inside her for eternity. When we made love, my world seemed instantly restored to some level of normality and tonight was no exception.

At least for the moment.

That night had given me cause to take stock, to really take time to think about this beautiful girl with whom I had fallen in love. We always celebrated our three months, four months and then five-month anniversaries with sumptuous romantic dinners, followed by exquisite love making, which cemented our connection. I was drinking and eating and enjoying life. But my eyes were not shut to certain realities that kept encroaching into our perfect world.

She wouldn't eat and constantly skipped meals and then would always be drinking at dinner, at bars, at restaurants and with our friends. Not just one or two mind you, Simone would continue to drink until there was no more. And strangely it never seemed to affect her. I knew this was an issue but thought it could be worse.

I raised the matter delicately one time and was met with the response:

"Don't be stupid, I love a drink, I'm Italian, and we all drink like this!"

Call me old fashioned, but I think it's more the catch cry of an alcoholic.

THIRTEEN

9th December - Day 149

Tis the season

As the weeks rolled on my commitment to Simone stabilised and grew stronger. Our weekends continued to be sublime as we enjoyed our time together as all couples do. As the year moved inevitably to a close I suggested again that we consider taking a short holiday together over Christmas. I could roll a couple of leave days together and end up with a week of leave to spend with her. I knew she was going home to see her family, but I was hoping we could have our own quick mini-Christmas getaway, either before she left or once she returned.

She said it was a good idea but it was her reaction to my suggestion that really left its mark. There was an awkwardness, an almost evasiveness to her response. She quickly changed the subject and the moment was lost. I remember feeling disappointed that she had not embraced this suggestion with the enthusiasm I felt it deserved. This was our end of year; this was our first Christmas and New Year. Apart from her mum, who else would she want to be with other than me?

9 December

> Feel secure in the knowledge that what we have is so special, nothing can change or come between us.
> I'm sorry I won't be here with you during Christmas, believe me if I could, I would be by your side in an instant. But my mother needs me right now.
> When I return we will start our life together properly.
> Sharing a home and committing to the love we have forged over the last few months.
> I am yours and you are mine my darling!!! ♡ ♡
> 8.17am

Before the issue of holidays, or lack thereof, could gather any momentum and before I could press the issue, circumstances overtook the discussion. I remember that she had been telling me how ill her grandmother was and that she feared that her decline would become acute. Her mother had told her in a recent discussion that her grandmother was deteriorating and she feared the worst.

Her fears were fulfilled one Saturday morning in the middle of December when she received a phone call from her mother telling her that her grandmother had passed away that morning. I tried as best as I could to console her, but her reaction was to seek isolation and she asked to be left alone. She went for a long walk by herself and said she would return as soon as she felt better which turned out to be later that afternoon.

14 December

> Words r hard to find in these
> situations.
> U may feel very alone at the
> moment, in a country so far
> away from your roots and family.
> Please know that I love u
> profoundly and am grieving with
> u. May u have a long life full of
> joy and happiness, and I pray
> that I may play a role in your
> future All my love, your Michael
> xxx
> 9.27am

Within a day or two of learning of the news of her grandmother's passing she suddenly announced.

"I have decided to go home for the whole of my Christmas holidays now. I need to be with my mother. I'm sorry, I know you had other ideas for us, but I need to focus on my family right now", and with that she walked away. The discussion was over. In fact there was no discussion, but merely a statement of fact. Again I thought it strange that she hadn't asked me whether I would like to come with her, however, I didn't press it as I thought it was part of her grieving and I still felt she had not fully accepted me as part of 'her' family.

I knew she was still receiving phone calls from her 'ex'; sometimes she would even tell me about them. It made me feel more and more uncomfortable but I didn't raise concern because I didn't want her to feel I doubted her, or even worse, suspected her. I said it was my hope one day that I could meet her ex and that as strange as it might seem we might actually have some sort of social relationship. She said that would be wonderful but right now it just wouldn't work and I left the topic in abeyance. I remember saying to her:

"Simone this may seem crazy to you, but I don't think he has

121

given up on you, he calls you, he emails you and this sort of dependency seems unhealthy and excessive." She didn't answer when I raised this but just looked down nodding her head.

"I wouldn't be at all surprised if he is heading back to Italy too for Christmas." I said...and sure enough.

14 December

So guess who has also decided to go home for Christmas this year? Marco hasn't been there for years. I'm not sure why this even surprises me... Part of me wants to cancel, and I would if it wasn't for my mum.... I love you!!!
7.40am

Didn't I tell u!!!!!! Can u call ????
Can we meet for a coffee???
7.43am

Are you ok?
10am

Not brilliant, need a hug, any hugs available??? When can we talk?
10.05am

What's to discuss? Marco will be in town when I am there. It's out of my control!!!! Let it go. I couldn't care less where he is.
10.08am

She had told me that over the last seven years their families in Italy had become quite close. In fact, their mothers had become good friends. I had suspected that if Simone was returning home for Christmas that news would have travelled fast between the two mothers and if there was a forlorn hope there could be some form of reconciliation attempted, then that would be the time to undertake this sort of discussion.

"You have to be joking, don't be so stupid!" she said vehemently, shutting me down. Her reaction was strong, but in my mind, I thought she was in complete denial.

She now said this was an excellent opportunity for her to tell the families that they had broken up and that there was no longer any possibility of reconciliation.

"I promise I will tell my mother and his mother that I have met the most amazing man, and I want nothing more than to continue my relationship with him. Anyhow Marco is seeing a woman he met in Singapore."

Simone said she knew her; she was from Sydney, and from memory, seemed to be a lovely woman. Once again my concerns were appeased and I thought, I will let them sort it out amongst themselves and she will come back with the matter finally resolved.

15 December

How is the expedition??
3.16pm

I'm walking home now via Aldi.xoxo
3.17pm

See u about 4.30??xxx
3.18pm

I need to be alone. Right now I'm cracking under the pressure of going home, of you not trusting me. And how's this? Marco is here for work and has organised for us to fly together??? honestly...right now all I want is to escape somewhere on my own, where I don't know anyone, and I don't have to please everyone or anyone. I'll call you later.
3.25pm

Now u tell me, I could tell these arrangements have been affecting u. I can sense that these things r affecting u. And I have to say whether u accept it or not, he still has some hold on u. However, he can't undo what we mean to each other. I love u, but u have to learn to talk to me. I am actually a little disappointed that u haven't told me. Can u understand?
3.45pm

No honestly, I don't understand. I told you as soon as I found out, which is NOW... I can't win.. Understand???
4.00pm

No
4.10pm

R u home?
4.01pm

I would like to walk over and see u. I need to talk... Xxx
4.15pm

I'll be home in 30 mins.
4.16pm

Ok, love u and see u soon xoxo
4.16pm

Can you bring the shampoo and
the umbrella please!!
4.17pm

We met at her place as agreed and talked through everything that seemed to be causing Simone so much grief and stress.

I can't begin to thank you for
persevering with me.
You force me to talk, and I need
to do that. I shut down when
things get too much.
I promise you this...next year is
our year, and I will do everything
in my power to ensure you and I
are the priority.
I guess I get scared that this
bubble of perfection is about to
burst. I don't help matters when
I shut down, and the worst thing
is, I know I'm doing it, but I have
no control over it. I saw
something today that reminded
me of how perfect you are for
me, so I bought it. I will give it to

you this weekend.
I love you!!!!♡ ♡ ♡
7.00pm

Thank u
7.03pm

125

Sooooo, I have just finished a very lengthy and detailed discussion with my mum.
She is now completely up to date with me, you, us and what happened with Marco.
She cried. She was so happy for me. She can hear in my voice how happy I am.
She loved Marco, but has over the years, sensed my unhappiness. I cannot tell you how light and happy
I feel right now. All because of you.
I love you!!!!!!!! ♡♡♡
11.34pm

16 December

Wow !!! Good morning !! I am so glad to have read this!!! That is wonderful and should set the tone for your visit!!! I love u more and more !!! Xoxoxo
6.56am

We met that day for a beautiful romantic lunch at China Doll. The sun was shining, the champagne was flowing, and as I looked at my girl, I was left breathless. When desert was served, I took Simone's hand and I looked directly in her eyes. I told her without a doubt in my mind, that she was the woman for me. Her eyes welled up with tears, and she squeezed my hand tightly. I then pulled out a beautiful ring and slid it on her finger. I said this was not a proposal... yet... but something to remind her of me, whilst she was across the seas at Christmas. She was so overwhelmed with emotion, I loved seeing her so happy. She got up and came and sat on my lap and kissed me with such tenderness. We were lost in our own little world, until we realized that the tables around us started to clap. We were both beaming, and perhaps slightly embarrassed at the commotion we had caused in the restaurant. The rest of the afternoon was spent strolling in the sun, arm in arm. It was perfect.

I love the ring! Thank you thank you thank you!!!! But I love you more!!!!!
5.17pm

FOURTEEN

19th December - Day 153

Storage

I thought I would make the best of the short vacation over Christmas and I booked a holiday with my daughter to travel to the Margaret River district in Western Australia. I had never been there and had been told by many people that it was simply the land of 'milk and honey.' So ultimately everything had been resolved, and we would spend nine days apart and she promised with every breath that her love for me was un-shakable. I believed her, but admittedly, I felt disappointed and a little empty that I had not been included in any of the planning.

A few days before she was due to leave we were at dinner talking, laughing and enjoying the warm glow of two lovers who could create their own world in any environment. At the end of dinner I offered to walk her home as I normally would and had before. Again, she protested and said no she would go by herself. As it was late, she insisted that I catch a taxi. As I got into the taxi I again felt a strange sense of unease. I had developed the ability to sense her movements, her moods, her intonation and most of all her eyes.

I could actually look into her eyes and see what she was thinking.

No sooner had I arrived back home when I received a text from her. She was extremely embarrassed and upset with her behaviour; she explained the reason was that Marco had sent some more of his stuff for her to store and that she didn't want me to see his belongings lying around in her apartment. Was this Groundhog Day?

Had we not had this exact event happen only a week or so ago? Initially my reaction was one of amazement, what sort of a person would send his clothes and belongings to her for storage? And this was the second time he had done this.

"You are being used can't you see it?" I implored.

"Yes but this is what he does" and she apologised and said how much she loved me. I continued to develop a feeling of unease. There was something that didn't seem right, I could sense it, but I accepted every explanation and she disarmed me with kisses and proclamations of love.

There was a distinct pattern emerging in our relationship where her behaviour would knock me off balance and then there would be the 'confessional' conversation, which led to forgiveness – but there was always a new affront.

She now told me that he had felt so sorry for her over her grandmother's passing that he was buying them both business class air tickets to Italy. He would come to Sydney and they would fly together. I didn't know how to react...my mind was spinning. I knew I didn't want to overreact, but I knew something was wrong. Didn't she realise how this could compromise her in my eyes? Didn't she realise that she was being bought for the sake of a lousy air ticket? And again and again I was met with the same responses.

"You have to understand, we have been together for eight years, and we are very good friends; almost family, just like you and Miriam. You have to understand this and you have to trust me. I love you so much, but this is getting tiresome"

And so I left it at that, chiding myself for being like an insecure teenager. I expected her to embrace my family, my past, my ex. Why couldn't I return the favour? It didn't help that I had never met Marco, maybe if I had met him; I would be able to witness their interaction myself and dispel these fears and thoughts of the two that constantly attacked my consciousness. I guess deep in my heart part of me couldn't believe that this beautiful young blonde, almost 20 years my junior, wanted to spend her life with me; had moved countries to be with me. My delicate bubble was close to perfect, and I couldn't stand for it to burst.

FIFTEEN

21st December - Day 155

Departure Take 1

Finally, the day before her departure I arrived to say goodbye. She said she was catching up with a girlfriend that evening and had to pack so I arrived at her apartment about 4.00pm with a surprise present for her mother. I had also bought her another ring from the Mont Blanc shop. Yes another ring. It had a lot more meaning than the first one but it was still not an engagement ring. It was however a beauty – stainless steel and rose gold. I said this was my present for her for Christmas and I wanted her to wear it and to know that when she had it on, I would be with her. She looked at it with the eyes of the six-year-old who had just been presented with a beautiful ice cream. She opened the box flipped open the lid and stared.

"This is so beautiful" she said and then couldn't help but repeat it over and over "this is so beautiful!" She took the ring in the hand. "I love it! I love it! And I love you so much." She burst into tears and repeated that she loved me so much and her mother would be thrilled.

We talked and we hugged and we said goodbye. I walked out of the block, but once again, with a strange sense of unease. For all her faults I loved her in a way that scared me. My mind said this is only a few days and she would be back and we could start planning our lives together.

21 December

> Good night and sleep tight. Have a safe and wonderful trip. Know that u go with my heart and all my love Xxxxx
> 9.17pm

> Thank u my darling, I'm sorry that lately I've been a nutter, but I feel so strongly connected to you, that I can't wait to get back, and get on with OUR lives together. You have been my rock and have stood by me unwavering in your love and commitment to me.
> I doubt I would have been so patient with someone who had such big mood swings. I'll text you in the morning.
> I love you desperately. ♡ ♡ ♡
> 9.34pm

My heart ached at the prospect of an empty Christmas and New Year. So I turned my energies towards my daughter and thought this would be a wonderful opportunity to spend quality time with her – unfortunately something I had not done enough in the past.

The next morning I woke to texts from Simone telling me they were at the airport and waiting to board. My heart sank, it was real. She was leaving and Marco was by her side.

22 December

Hey Darling, well you wouldn't believe it!!
The flight has been delayed.
Typical Christmas travelling....aggghhhhh
6.35am

Good morning, Oh no!! Well at least the airport is not closed. Well I hope it's not too long..
Love u!!!
7.13am

So we are not going anywhere. Engine not working and the flight is completely cancelled. oh well, guess it's better to find out now than in the air!! May get on another airline, but not hopeful. ♡
7.21am

So my none too patient travelling companion won't wait at the airport till this arvo, so we are on another flight tomorrow.
Heading home, and guess who is staying at my place? least I can do after he paid for my ticket.
We will be returning at same time tomorrow morning...note to self, no more OS trips at xmas.
Love you! ♡
7.40am

Oh no!!! Do u want to come here???? It's not going to be very comfortable, in more ways than

one !! R u coming back home now??!
Keen to have breakfast together?
7.45am

UMMMM, I don't think so. More for Marco's sake. You get it, I'm sure.
Please don't worry about me tonight.
You have to be able to trust me. We actually had an amazing talk this morning about you. It was really positive and I feel comfortable hanging out with him.
8.00am

My reaction was one of elation I felt like a prisoner who had been granted clemency... Another day together... We could go for a walk, have lunch, and make love for the last time. As I was contemplating all the activities that could provide us with a few more stolen moments my world came to a shuddering, astonishing halt. Her next text nonchalantly announced that she had arranged to go sailing with a friend of hers who had access to a maxi yacht on Sydney Harbour!

Yes if course I trust u!!! But I think that it's an imposition on his part.
Plus he can pick up the cost on his travel insurance for a hotel!
Do u want to come for a blended juice this morning?
8.03am

Let me go home first ok, I'll text you later.
8.10am

Ok xxx
8.11am

22 December

> When does sailing finish?? We r at the cute Italian café just down from u, U r welcome to join us! X
> 9.57am

Michael, I forgot to tell you with all the preparations of departing, and thinking it wasn't going to eventuate, that Jules asked me yesterday to come out on one of the Sydney to Hobart super yachts with her. I've just left a message saying I'm available if there is still a spot left.
8.05am

> Wow!!! I am available!!!!! Xxx
> 8.09am

I'll ask Xoxo
8.09am
Only room for me Xoxo
8.11am

You're kidding??!! Just walked by a few minutes ago, didn't see you. Just grabbing supplies for the boat. Heading there around 11-ish to meet the team. I'm guessing we will be on the harbour all day. I'm so excited
10.08am

> Ok, sounds fantastic!!! Take lots of pics. Call me when u finish!!xx
> 10.12am

I remember standing shocked at the text, my first and only thought...what about me? What am I? Chopped liver? I didn't react I didn't want to sound unreasonable, grasping or insecure. But I began to die on the inside.

She rang at lunchtime I could tell she had been drinking. She told me how much she loved me and that I could trust her because she and Marco and a group of friends were going out for dinner. She kept repeating that I shouldn't worry and nothing will happen between her and Marco. Again she re-iterated that it was an emergency and they were just good friends. My heart sank and I accepted her explanation but I knew there was something wrong and her behaviour was appalling. I was so hurt that she would spend her last day in Sydney without me.

> Any plans tonight? xoxo
> 1.00pm

I am having dinner with u ♡ ♡
1.03pm

> Hi can u call please? Xxx
> 5.35pm

Is Marco there??
5.36pm
Is he going for dinner??
5.37pm

> Yes, the whole boat is going. It was such an amazing day. Wish you could've been there. You would've loved it.
> Thinking of you xoxo
> 6.05pm

"Wish I was there?" ." I would've loved it?" Are you kidding me? I wish I had been there too but apparently there was only room on the boat for her....and somehow a miraculous spare spot became available for Marco and now they were all continuing the party on shore together. I was not invited at any point to join in. I was confused and somewhat speechless. Her words in the texts didn't match her actions. I felt so alone at that moment.

A few hours later she called me again. It was obvious she had drunk considerably more since our previous call at lunchtime. I was out to dinner with my daughter, and she kept asking me to tell her that I loved her. I thought at the time that she was being so childish. It wasn't appropriate to gush like a silly teenager in front of Naomi, and I wasn't quite feeling the love like she was. I wasn't sure how I was feeling.

> Are you ashamed to profess your love to me in front of Naomi?
> I say it loudly and proudly in front of anyone and everyone.
> We must be at different stages of love huh?
> Anyway... I'll leave you to it. I'm off to bed... Love you xoxo
> 8.55pm

> Well I do love u!!! It's just that I am telling her about how I feel about u now!!! She hasn't met u yet!! I just need to be a little understated. I hope u understand!! Love you! ♡ ♡ ♡
> 9.10am

Just got home. Had a very lovely talk to Naomi. I was explaining to her how love had found her father again, and that it was wonderful and how u know when u meet someone that u trust with your life. Sounds like u had a wonderful day on our beautiful Harbour!!!! Please have a great time os and please tell your mother what I said... ♡ ♡
9.30pm

I miss you so much already. It's weird being so close, yet so far from each other. Sorry for being a drunken idiot earlier. I just needed to hear you say the words. I can't wait to be back in your arms!!!?? Xoxo
9.45pm

Get a good night Sleep!!! Safe flight Xxxx
9.50pm

On my way home. Can't wait to fall into bed. Let's organize a meet and greet with Naomi when I get back.
I need the tick of approval from Daddy's little girl, or we will never work!! lol
I'm not sure how I'm going to manage without you for 2 weeks. It makes me feel sick in my tummy... My worst fear is you will forget about me and find someone amazing to replace me......can't bear to think that way.
I love you Michael Sherman xoxox
10.15pm

23 December

Ok....so let's try this departing thing again shall we??? lol Have a fabulous time away with Naomi. You will be in my heart every second of every minute of every hour of every day we are apart. Bon Voyage baby xoxo
6.31am

Good morning!! Good luck take 2!! Hope u have a wonderful trip too!! U r in my heart. I miss u already 🤍
6.39am

Is the plane ok??? Xxx
6.51am

Yes all good to go I think
6.52am

Great ... A safe trip ... Xoxox
6.53am

Just boarded, love you! I'll be back on the 5th. Can't wait!!!!🤍🤍
7.10am

Have a great flight, watch some good movies!!! I love u and miss u terribly already. Xxxx
7.12am

Same!!!! Can't live without you anymore🤍🤍
7.13am

141

She had given me a present for Christmas, a key ring, and she had had the ring inscribed with the words… 'The journey ends…' She had bought the same keyring and her counterpart was also inscribed… 'Where lovers meet'.

She had remembered the poem I had coined for her some weeks before. I had borrowed some Shakespeare and added my own embellishment and the poem read:

"The journey ends where lovers meet, provided there is no deceit, let hearts reach out and souls declare… You are my destination."

SIXTEEN

25th December - Day 159

Merry Christmas!!

HELLOOOOOOOO!!!!!

From the moment she disappeared into 'the holiday' to Italy, I felt there had been a great dislocation to my life. Something just did not feel right. Her behaviour on the day of her departure was inexplicable, yet whilst she had professed absolute and unconditional love for me, she had effectively dumped me for a day of sailing and dinner with Marco and friends. Her pathetic phone call to me whilst I was with my daughter was soaked in alcohol, and for the very first time I felt that she was being disingenuous.

I pondered over these matters whilst I was high in the clouds on the way to Western Australia and as is my tendency, I analysed everything to the point of exhaustion. I knew something was wrong. I just couldn't put my finger on it, so denied the reality and told myself I had to trust her and all would be revealed when she returned.

I had to trust her!

My holiday with Naomi was magnificent. I was able to talk to my daughter the way a father does when he recognises his little girl is now growing up into a mature young woman. We talked about her new love interest, which provided great therapy for me and took my mind off the fact I'd heard nothing from my love interest for 48 hours.

25 December

> Good morning and merry
> Xmas!!!
> I hope today is a joyous day for u
> and your mother!!! Hope your
> mum likes the present!!! This is a
> picture of our view. We r in the
> middle of nowhere!! I miss u
> terribly.
> It actually hurts...Your Michael
> xxx
> 10.03am

She had told me that her mobile plan had only limited access to the Internet yet as I understand it, they have a number of telephones in Italy and she was certainly able to get access to a landline for the purposes of calling me, if indeed she had wanted to.

Meanwhile, Naomi and I toured the wine country and beaches and generally enjoyed our stay. I finally received a cryptic text from her declaring that she was going crazy as she had not heard from me! I was so relieved to hear from her, and once again I threw my doubts into the denial bin. She announced that she had gone skydiving near Milan!

29 December

OHHHH MAN!!!!! Jumped out of a plane today. So amazing. I screamed like a banshee all the way down. They let me do it again free of charge. What an amazing experience. Sending through some photos, I have a video to show you when I'm back. My cheeks are still glowing from being pelted by the rain as we fell at 200km/h. It was like being hit with a high powered tattoo gun.
How's the wine country? bring home some nice reds. I Love you, missing you xoxo
4.14pm

Wow, so happy u enjoyed the jump. I felt like that when u got out of the taxi that day!!! So beautiful here and wine is superb!!! Love u more!!! Really miss our passion :((
5.15pm

30 December

Hey, how are you? I'm having a great time catching up with old, old friends I haven't seen for over 10 years. Some are married, some with kids, some divorced. So glad I haven't gone down the kids path... not my thing really. They don't get it, but I do. Thank God you don't want any more!!!! heading back to mum tomorrow. Nothing planned for NYE. Not into big parties over here. Just quality time with my mum.

Hope you're enjoying
Margaret River xoxo
9.00am

Hi!!! Yes I have the order
forms!!!
Better to ship than to carry!!! R u
there?? I can call for a minute?? I
am glad that u r re-connecting
with your friends!!! Miss u!!!
When do u arrive?? Xoxox
11.30am

Naomi and I returned to Sydney just in time for New Year's Eve. I received a New Year's Eve text but my enthusiasm was starting to drain away.

Change of plans...I have decided
to come home via New
Zealand....am flying to
Queenstown and will stay with
my old Singapore friends Gillian
and Albert. I will do all the
outdoor stuff!! Bungy jumping,
kayaking!! Miss U. xx
8.12pm

Then the text that really began my descent into misery arrived. There was no invitation to join her, no explanation as to how she had been able to arrange this excursion at short notice. She explained that she was tired of what she called 'small town' Italy even though she had been able to catch up with a number of school friends.

2 January

Have u jumped out of any
planes??
1.14pm

LOL... Been there.... done that. Moving on to new adventures. Drum roll... White water rafting. Water is freezing!! Are you flying back home today? Xoxo
1.20pm

Am home!!! Wonderful break. Sydney 35!!! Miss u terribly. Am I allowed to say that?? Xx
1.22pm

Are you kidding? I'd be upset if you weren't missing me. I'll send you a video of me bungee jumping. Love you!!! xoxo
1.25pm

Take care, I need u fit and well!!!
Xo
1.28pm

About to get on raft. Do you still love me??? Xoxo
1.29pm

Do you??
1.31pm

Of course I love you. You are my everything. I miss you terribly, and I can't wait to begin our lives together as soon as you get back! Your Michael xoxoxoxo
1.33pm

Thank you....when I'm with you, I have no doubts about how you feel, but as soon as we are apart, I think you have lost interest. It's nothing you do or say, just my own insecurities. Cannot wait for your embrace on Sunday. Here's the bungee picture xoxo
4.30pm

I really wanted to encourage her to have a great time but I felt so empty and cheated that she was undertaking all these activities without me. Yet her texts still professed absolute love and devotion towards me. It's as if her words had been disconnected from her actions. I had been cut out of her life.

The whole reason for going away was to spend quality time with her mother and reconnect with her family. That I understood, but to return to Australia via New Zealand for some fun and adventure and not think about inviting me, hurt me deeply. Was I being over sensitive? What was happening??

SEVENTEEN

3rd January - Day 168

You're Where? With Who?!

The next day I returned to work. Instead of feeling relaxed and re-energised after my break I was actually in a state of acute anxiety. I had invested every emotion within me for this woman, but somehow I felt empty degraded and drained – as if it were a premonition.

I remember walking in Martin Place about 2.00 pm on the Thursday before her return to Sydney. I was feeling a little bit better because suddenly we were back in constant communication. The texts were flowing and she was professing to have missed me terribly. I told her that I was so sad to have missed New Year's Eve with her and couldn't wait for her to return. I explained I would be more than delighted to pick her up from the airport when she returned. I joked that's what real boyfriends do!

3 January

Can't wait to see u. When is your flight landing??? Can I pick u up??X
9.14am

And then the first bomb dropped.

> Its ok sweetheart, thanks for the offer, but Marco will drop me home.
> Saves you the hassle of coming to the airport and having to park.
> I'll call as soon as I'm back on Sunday.
> Love you !!! xoxo
> 11.39am

I remember stopping in the street and staring at this text so, she WAS with him! He was in New Zealand with her!!

My mind raced, my reaction was simple. How could she have planned a holiday with her ex-boyfriend and left me behind in Sydney? I had only just started to comprehend the text when another one rolled in... a second more devastating bomb...

She wanted me to see a photo of her bungee jump. She made a comment that I was not to stir her about her strange style in the fall. She said I'll send you a photo immediately and we can laugh about it when I return. Within seconds an entire photo album arrived on my iPhone; a 'drop box app' collection. I opened it and was immediately greeted with a photograph that sickened me. There they were!! The two of them standing together on the bungee platform smiling and grinning. There was even a video of the two of them!!

> Can u call me immediately
> 11.41am

> How could u do this to me??
> 11.44am

> Do what to you???
> 11.45am

> U knew exactly what u were
> doing. U deceived me. And u
> sent me photos of u 2 together,
> as a 6 months anniversary
> present. U have devastated me.
> How can I ever trust u? Thank u
> for ruining my holiday.
> 11.47am

> If u can't understand how I feel
> then there is no hope. I'm so
> upset. Today is our 6 months
> anniversary
> 11.49am

> I had such a surprise. ... Hah
> U have broken my heart.
> 11.50am

> U treated me so badly the day u
> left.
> 11.51am

The rage within me was building with every second. The phone rang and she asked me if I was okay? I spat out the word no, and immediately launched into a tirade. She tried to explain that she had sent me a text telling me that Marco was going to accompany her to New Zealand, but conveniently, and not surprisingly, I hadn't received it. I told her that it just didn't wash with me. I told her that her text about the change of travel plans never mentioned him.

"How could you do this? I should be there with you." Then she openly admitted that she knew that if she had told me he was coming she knew that I would be extremely upset.

For me this was the admission that made me feel all the more justified in my reaction and the anger that was seething within me. In my mind I knew something had gone terribly wrong. She had deceived me and planned this trip with him.

I hung up before I unleashed my fury on her. I didn't want to say something I could possibly regret, but right at that moment, I thought her to be the most despicable being in the world, and I couldn't trust my anger to filter my emotions with any level of civility.

She then sent a long ambling text yet again explaining herself. The pattern was clearly re-emerging, and Marco was forever the constant life force that inhabited our relationship like a festering boil threatening to burst its foulness all over what I considered to be our pristine love.

> Michael you have to believe me when I say that this is a misunderstanding, and that somehow my texts informing you that Marco was also going to be in NZ were lost. Maybe holiday traffic and the airwaves were congested? I DON'T KNOW how it happened, but I did send them. Why would I continue to tell you

> that I love you, and that you are my everything if I still had feelings for him?
> It just doesn't make sense. I would be with him if that was the case.
> Besides, he has met a girl in Singapore. I want to be with you, make a life with you, wake up with you every day, do everything with you. I love you completely and wholly.
> I don't know what else I can tell you. I made a mistake by not telling you.
> You will break my heart if you leave me. I have just tried to get on a plane today, but there is nothing available.
> What have I done? Please believe me!!
> 12.27pm

My response was decisive, analytical and cold.

This was not a misunderstanding. U deceived me and u knew it, u have been weird for weeks, and it's all because of him. I am so upset. How could u do this to me? I was reading the love letter I sent u. I feel so humiliated. U said once that u wouldn't like to be in my shoes with all your mood swings, well try them on now!!!
I trusted u completely without reservation. U sent a knife through my heart . U knew how I would feel about this and u hid it from me, my head is aching. People who really love each other don't plan such elaborate deceptions, and rub salt into the wound. Telling me I can't pick u

up from the airport!!!! Because moneybags has a limo to take you back to his hotel! I feel sick.
12.30 pm

And just so u understand it is not jealousy, I just feel that u deceived me, and to be with him. Can't u understand!!!!!!!
12.31 pm

I get it. I know exactly how it looks, and if it was reversed, I'd be feeling the same as you. Yet again I have disappointed you and probably lost the best thing that has ever happened to me. If I could change my mistakes I would. I never intentionally meant to hurt you. I'm sorry. That's all I can say. I will give you back the jewelery you have so generously given me. I deserve nothing.
You are too good for me. Again I'm sorry !!!
12.34pm

How do u think I feel when I see this?? Sick in the stomach
12.35pm

I emailed the photo of the two of them smiling on the Bungee platform.

He has got a new girlfriend!!!
12.35pm

I sent the photo again, as if to say – "Yes, he certainly has!" The image of them together almost made me vomit.

Michael please!
12.40pm

Well she should be there, and u
should be with me
12.49pm

Yes you are absolutely right!!!!!
A decision I will live with and
regret for the rest of my life!
12.50pm

I could have gone there, if I had
been invited!! I flew half way
round the world to rescue u. I
thought you were with your
friends in Italy until yesterday. I
could have taken a plane over
there, I checked, but I wasn't
even invited
12.51pm

If you will please let me explain
face to face?
12.52pm

I wasn't a damsel in distress!!!
I made a decision to relocate,
and yes, you were an integral
part of my decision making, and
yes, I moved quicker than I
probably would have because of
you... but you didn't rescue me!!!
12.55pm

I will pick u up at the airport,
that's what a real couple do, if
that is embarrassing then there
is nothing to talk about.
12.56pm

As soon as I know which flight
I'm on I'll let you know arrival
times.
12.58pm

Earlier the better, but if u r on the booked ticket I will pick u up ok ?
1.00pm

Promise me you won't yell at me. I couldn't handle it. I'm so upset already.
1.05pm

U better think about how u have hurt me, and how u have been acting, this has been going on for weeks. I expect total honesty. I would never shout at u in public. Do u realize how u treated me the day before I left ???? U were horrible. U couldn't make time for a good bye kiss cause u were too busy with him.. Again!!!
1.07pm

I have never done anything to hurt u but Marco is the one who cheated on u and destroyed your life. Well he gets top priority!!!
1.08pm

Do u have any idea how I feel???? I think u do
1.10pm

Of course I do...I think it's best if you don't pick me up. I can see I've hurt you too much.
I have completely messed up. I'm an idiot.
1.12pm

Do u think I am a moron? U keep asking me, do I still love u? Do u think I am stupid???
1.13pm

Do u want me to
pick u up or not???
1.14pm

It appears I'm the stupid one.
I am the moron and I'm now
paying the price for my stupidity.
I'll get a cab.
1.16pm

Tell me the flight details when u
get them please. Do u want me?
If u do then u have to rebuild my
trust, and u have to be honest.
Because as I have suspected he
has some sort of hold on u .
I'm sorry to say. And u know it.
1.17pm

I am sitting here contemplating
that I met u exactly 6 months
ago.Tonight is our anniversary,
and I have never felt so empty.
Thank u for ruining it.
Actions speak louder than words.
For all the "I love u's" amount to
nothing when u deceive
someone.
5.26pm

I'm not going to text anymore
until we see each other. It's only
making things worse. I love you. I
do.
And whatever you think about
me going home with Marco, it
was actually a positive
experience for everyone. For
him, you, me, us and our
families. Everything was laid out
on the table and our families
were very understanding and
supportive.
Yes going to NZ was stupid, and I
can only pray that I have not lost

157

you forever as a result. The last 6 months have seen me grow and mature into someone I would hope you would be proud to be with. I've never been happier. To think that what we have is over... kills me!!!! I'm on an earlier flight on Sunday so will arrive in the afternoon.
If you will lend me an ear, I would like to sit with you and tell you everything.... about my past. It is time for you to hear the whole truth about me.
9.10pm

I deserve nothing less than the truth. I thought we had an agreement that we were to tell each other everything..... Why have u not ???
10.03pm

I thought we agreed that nothing would come between us. I was very upset today. I have had a pain in my stomach for hours. Do u think I don't feel your pain???
10.05pm

You need to know that I never cheated on you, nor even thought about it. I'm not sure if that's maybe playing in your head? You are the one I love and you are the one I want to spend the rest of my life with. I feel that I'm being wrongly accused, because I know I sent you through a text explaining he was going to be in NZ visiting friends. It was a coincidence.
Why would I send you through photos of us if I was trying to

hide anything?
10:07 pm

Could this have been possible? I could not accept the possibility, or the convenience of lost texts.

I don't want to say anything rash.
I never received that text.
I have hardly had any texts.
10.09pm

I am so distressed. My friends know something is wrong, but I feel if I open up, I will lose it and become an emotional mess.
I just want to be swallowed up. I wish I was somewhere else right now. For what its worth... I love you !!!!
10.11pm

It seems you didn't get a lot of my texts.
Like the one saying how much my mum loved your gift, The 'I miss You so Much' texts. 'That we had told our families' etc, etc
10.14pm

Do u realize how much of a shock this was? And I think this New Zealand trip was organised a while back??
10.17pm

The whole thing has been a disaster
10.18pm

I swear to you it wasn't!!!!
10.21pm

Please let me talk to you face to face?
10.22pm

I will pick u up at the airport. And we can talk
10.26pm

At this stage, I'm arriving at 4.50pm, unless I get on standby. will let you know. I'm going to bed.
10.27pm

Ok.. Go to bed and get some rest... Are u in a hotel??
10.28pm

No, in my friends campervan. I miss you so much!!
10.30 pm

PS That doesn't mean I regret coming here with him....
10.31 pm

I don't understand the last sentence??
10.33pm

Who?
10.36pm

Oh God!!!! I meant to say...I regret coming here with Marco!!!
10.37pm

That makes 2 of us. So I am going to bed. We can talk in the morning.
10.38pm

Good night! I love you....
10.45pm

She had pleaded with me and tried to convince me that she loved me and she had no doubt in her mind that she wanted to be with me. She admitted to having made a terrible mistake; one that could quite possibly be very costly. She would catch an earlier plane home and said she would explain everything. I was shattered. I was lost. I was confused.

I felt it necessary to confide in a number of friends, just to see if I was justified in how I was responding and how I was feeling. They were speechless. They could not believe this petite, sophisticated, intelligent woman was capable of such devious actions.

I even spoke to her best friend who couldn't believe how stupid she had been. I later found out Peta had also told her how disappointed she was in her behaviour and terminated their friendship.

There were no excuses. This was simply inexcusable and for me it was the descent into a world of mistrust and suspicion which would continue to envelope me like an ill- fitting coat.

EIGHTEEN

4th January - Day 169

Slow Death

That night I tossed and turned and slept poorly. I tried to put together the pieces of this puzzle and work out what were all the possibilities that could have led to this. Obviously, Marco had not given up, I concluded that he must have attempted to bribe her with a trip to New Zealand and was attempting to reconcile with her. That must be the explanation. What else could be logical?

And then another text that rocked me to my core.

See??? why is this happening??? and now of all times? I have sent you 3 today. I will just be straight with you, and let you know I suffered another breakdown/ collapse episode and have been brought to the hospital.
As I am texting you, I have a drip coming out of my arm. So to update you on flights....
I'm currently on the one that brings me in at 7pm, but am desperately wanting to get on

the one arriving at 4pm. I figure I may as well just arrive early at the airport, and wait for a possible standby. I'm actually sneakily texting you, as phone not allowed to be on. As soon as I'm out of here, I'll turn it back on.
6.47pm

She said in simple terms that since our argument she had stopped eating and drinking and on the morning after, had collapsed and had been taken to hospital. I was beside myself with panic and even contemplated flying over to New Zealand to bring her home. She sent me more gut wrenching texts professing love and apologising for her stupidity.

4 January

Hope you slept ok, just found a café with wifi. Did you get my texts this morning? I haven't heard from you. I was worried...
9.56am

I have received no texts, just this one. I had a rotten night. Do u have your flight details?
10.05am

I was driving when I got this, couldn't answer, what can I say ?? I am even more devastated ... Of course I care about u This is ripping my heart to pieces, and now that u r ill and I am not with u. I am in tears Please call me when u get a chance. We will talk everything through, we have too much to lose....
7.17pm

Which hospital r u at??
7.18pm

R they treating u well?
7.19pm

I'm fine, it's the usual stuff. I'm severely dehydrated, haven't been eating well, no sleep, and the stress from our ordeal has taken its toll on my body. They're keeping me in overnight. Can't decide which is worse, a hospital bed, or a single bunk in a campervan? They are looking after me really well. Thank you for your concern.
You cannot understand what that means to me. I have to turn phone back off.
I love you and god I miss you!!!!
8:36 pm

What hospital???
8.36pm

So happy ur feeling better sleep well.
8.36pm

Is there a phone in the room??
I will call.
8.39pm

I had heard nothing for over an hour. She wouldn't answer my questions. I was beside myself with grief and stress. WHAT WAS GOING ON???? Then finally I could see she was typing, but it was going on and on....

What is going on????
9.36pm

R u writing a book???
9.36pm

I have been thinking quite a lot as I sit here alone with my thoughts.
I think about your reaction, and your tone of voice towards me when we spoke.
I love you, but I feel that a line has been crossed, and I'm not sure we can ever cross back over it to what we had. Right now, at this very moment, I think it best if I just get home and settle in and contact you over the next few days. I know I'm not strong enough to face any form of conflict, or be under scrutiny from you. I can openly and honestly say, you are the love of my life, but I think it best we say goodbye. I have caused too much hurt and heartache. You DO NOT deserve to be treated in such a disrespectful way, and that is exactly how I have treated you recently. I have a lot of unresolved baggage that keeps rearing its ugly head, and you keep getting dumped with it. You deserve better. Any girl would be honored to have you call them your girlfriend/partner or wife.
I held that honor, but I carelessly threw it away.
I wish for nothing more in the world than to hold that title again. But I realise, I am too damaged to be that woman right now. I will contact you when I'm back. I'm not sure what else I can say.
9:42 pm

I need to know the truth, u owe me this. Now u send a message like this to rip me up more ??? I am not going to yell at u. I am over the anger. I don't want to hurt u. I will pick u up. Please don't argue .. I still love u ...
I am so sad
9.46pm

5 January

I have slept on this and I want to say that with real love comes the capacity to understand and to forgive, u know me don't u? I have never pretended to be perfect. I have told u everything about me. Don't u think that I can understand the issues that you may have??? Please tell me the flight u r on and I will be there. For u and for us.....
6.24am

My heart melted again, how could I be angry with her in these circumstances? She was ill and lying in a hospital bed on a drip. The next day she was able to organise her discharge and went straight to the airport. I was begging her to allow me to pick her up but she refused, she said that she wanted to go straight home and freshen up. I was counting the hours. She wouldn't give me the details of her flight.

5 January

I'm at the airport feeling like crap in every sense. This is not how I envisaged my return when I left. I'll contact you once I'm home. I need to get my head

around seeing you.
I feel like I'm constantly on the
edge of crying.
11.37am

I am trying to ring u. Please tell
me the flight time and airline. If u
understand my text this morning
then u know that u don't have to
worry how u look .
Can u ring me please??
11.39 pm

R u on the early flight??
11.40 am

U know I really don't think u
have ever been in love, because
when u love someone as much
as I love u, you don't care how
they look. U just want to be with
them. So please tell me the flight
details.
11.41am

If it was me, wouldn't u be
busting down doors
to help me??
11.49 pm

Can u please ring
before u board?
11.50 am

I was pleading into a cyber-void. I didn't hear from her again till later that afternoon. It was a torturous wait.

NINETEEN

5th January - Day 170

The Explanation

5 January

I'm back....
meet me at Double Bay beach.
3.10pm

Her return hit me like a bolt of lightning. Finally I would have the confrontation, and hear her explanation. I demanded from her the truth, the whole truth, and nothing but the truth. I left the apartment and walked down to the beach. It was about 15 minutes from my place and my mind was racing over and over, imagining the various scenarios that would make sense out of all this chaos. I said to myself... "Don't lose it, don't scream, just listen, it's her that has to do the explaining."

It was a beautiful day, the sun was shining, but my heart was numb. Finally I turned towards the beach, and started walking along the promenade. There in the distance sitting on a bench I could see her staring down at the ground. I walked up to her and she lifted her head and looked at me. I don't know why I said it, but I asked her to stand up and give me a hug! She jumped up and threw her arms around me. She hugged me with such strength and I could hear a slight sob.

"I love you so much. I'm so sorry, I'm so sorry. Please forgive me." Her words moved me. I didn't have it in me to cross-examine her.

"You have to tell me everything. Everything! I need to know why you did this." It took all my strength to stop my voice from revealing my true emotions. I was so close to tears. But I was determined not to break down. All I wanted was to hear her out.

"I will tell you everything and I will tell you some things that I have never told anybody in my life". She had stopped sobbing and took on a solemnity I had never seen before. I was intrigued. There WAS an explanation. I knew it.

Before I let her begin, I felt it necessary to point out my immediate slant on the events that had transpired in the last few weeks.

"I don't understand! You have been pushing back for weeks, acting strangely, never letting me into your life. I thought we were... a team... I thought we were... soul mates." At the mention of those last words. Simone's composure burst. She could no longer hold herself together. I had hit a nerve. The dam had opened and the tears were flooding down her face.

"I will tell you everything; you deserve to hear the truth"

"I am listening" was all that I could utter. I hated seeing her in this state, but part of me was still so numb, and I really didn't know how to handle her. I wasn't sure if I should touch her, hold her.

Through her sobbing her words tumbled out of her mouth and were tainted with such sadness that I had no doubt of her sincerity or the veracity of her explanation. She began by telling me that her father had been a terrible alcoholic and when she was young he would often hit her mother.

When these episodes occurred, she would be taken to her next-door neighbours who understood the situation and would look after her. They were a lovely couple; their house was full of love and music unlike hers which was full of violence and fear. The husband in this couple was considerably older than the wife. Her mother had told her a few weeks before Christmas that he had passed away. The widow was beside herself with grief and wanted to die.

She looked into my eyes and said "I love you so much Michael, but I started to think about our age difference, and I couldn't stand the thought of losing you. That's why I've been so strange. That's why I wanted more time away from Sydney, and when Marco suggested that I join him in New Zealand that's why I said yes. I am such a fool." I sat there speechless, my suspicions, my fears, the anxiety drifted into the ether. My heart reached out to her.

"And now I will tell you something that I have never told anyone, not Marco, not my mother, not anyone." She looked directly into my eyes. The intensity rocked me to my core. I didn't know what was coming. I took a deep breath and exhaled audibly, bracing myself for the worst.

"When I was 12 years old my father's best friend raped me." and with that loaded statement came a torrent of tears. She was crying uncontrollably. Her shoulders were heaving and she was struggling for breath. I felt helpless and could only offer her my arms; I cradled her like a baby, and caressed her face. I rocked her gently back and forth trying to soothe her. Time stopped and everything that had happened seemingly dissolved away with those words. My grip tightened around her, more than ever I needed to protect her, save her from all the injustices that had occurred in her life.

"It's all right now, you have finally told someone, and I am here with you" I stated with such ferocity. I wanted to convince her that her demons could be conquered and I was her valiant knight that would slay them and lead her to her place of safety and security.

She went on to explain that this abuse had lasted for two years and at the end of it she stopped eating and developed anorexia and bulimia. She told me she had fought these disorders all of her life and sometimes she had succeeded but often not. The disorders had returned which explained her eating and drinking habits and possibly could account for her mood swings. I told her that she needed to talk to a professional, someone who specialised in this sort of matter.

"As far as I'm aware there are wonderful results and cures available. I would be with you and we would do it together." I implored her to take my advice. Then feeling we had exhausted the topic, we got up and walked home holding hands.

I continued to reassure her that her journey would not be solo and that we were indeed a team; a team that would be able to conquer all difficulties. I promised her that we would give each other strength and that we would make it together. I couldn't offer her anything else other than the conviction of my word. I certainly had stressed it many times, and knew that I had stated my case and position very clearly.

She didn't stay with me that night, she said she was too weak from the ordeal in New Zealand but we talked all night and texted. I experienced profound relief. I knew everything now... or so I thought.

I felt as though I could trust her and that we would start again. But there was one issue that I could not face and denied the possibility that it could be true. I had looked at her arms and the top of her hands for the "tell-tale" signs of an IV drip. Having come from a medical family and understanding what is involved in the application of a saline drip, I knew there would have to be a bruise or at least some marking where plaster had been applied to hold the drip in place. I couldn't see any.
Maybe I just wasn't looking in the right place?
Everything else was so credible...I must have missed it.

TWENTY

SAME DAY

Jumping hurdles...

How did I feel?

Emotionally I was still numb. Strangely though, relaxed, but completely numb. The overwhelming passion and excitement that I had experienced in the lead up to Christmas however, was gone.

I was still hurt even with her explanation. If I was truly the man that she said I was, that is, the most important man in her life, then why was she jumping off a bungee platform with her ex-boyfriend? My brain told me this was just not logical, but my heart accepted her explanation and I could only feel pity and sorrow after she told me her story.

5 January

Everything feels so good right now. I knew once we spoke openly, face to face, things would be resolved. I love you more than anything!! ♡ ♡
9.27pm

Thank you for giving me the strength to tell you everything
9.29pm

Me too!!! ♡ ♡ ♡ sleep tight. Tomorrow is the beginning of our new life!! Xoxo
9.38pm

Texting with hearts and kisses again!!
9.39pm

Agreed, I definitely missed the hearts and kisses. It wasn't the same without!! ♡
9.40pm

Get some rest!!! Xoxoxo
9.41pm

I am so exhausted, I need to go to bed, but just need to call mum quickly to let her know I'm home safely.
Can't wait to be with you and build our future together! And I promise, there will be no more lies or secrets. I love you from the bottom of my heart Michael!! ♡ ♡ ♡
9.43pm

Agreed!!!!! Send my regards to your Mum!! Xoxoxox
9.44pm

6 January

Morning baby, wow didn't I have a good sleep, best in weeks. Dare say the relief I felt after our talk yesterday was enormous and no doubt was reason for such a

deep slumber. I love you so much! What are you doing tonight? ♡
6.31am

Morning!!! Yes best night for a loooooooong time!!!! No plans, what have u got in mind? Xoxo
6.57am

Just need to finish all my washing and then hang it up, then how about a really simple day, with walks, a lovely swim, cuddling, hand holding. lol....bit much? I just feel like I need to be close to you today. Tell you how much you mean to me and how lucky I am to have you ♡
6.59am

Yes, that sounds pretty good especially the last bit!! ♡ ♡ Please promise me that u will have something for brekky!X
7.03am

I promise sweetheart, I need some protein big time. As soon as I finish work, I'll come straight to you. Love you!!! Xoxo
7.06am

She seemed to recover her strength quickly. I was lecturing her regularly now on nutrition, the need to eat properly and regularly and she seemed to listen and accepted my advice. She said that she wanted to show me some photographs of her family and brought her iPad to my place so we could look together. She stayed over on the Tuesday evening after her Sunday return. We cooked and laughed and made love, and I started to think maybe, just maybe, things would get back to normal.

I cared deeply for her, so it was time to talk again about moving in together and beginning a proper life as a real couple. This was an exciting discussion and we reveled in the notion that we would redecorate together and travel to work together on the ferry. She told me she wasn't concerned any more about the age difference. I explained to her that age was just a number, and that she had to accept me as I was. If we had some great years together, it would be better than having none or being with a partner who made you miserable. She seemed to accept this, and even when we were making breakfast on the Wednesday morning, we were still capturing some of the joy that we had experienced only a couple of weeks ago before... 'The Trip'.

After breakfast she checked her iPhone and I could see her scrolling down her emails. One must have caught her attention because her face contorted and I knew it must have been serious because she rarely swore, "Oh shit!" she said.

"What's the matter?" I questioned her. She looked at me and said

"It's Marco. He wants me to look at properties for him."

I was gob smacked. It was now safe to say my immense dislike for this man had now turned to hate. He was the sole cause of all our disconnects.

"What are you going to do?" I asked, almost testing.
She said with determination

"He can look after his own bloody properties!"

She spat it out with such venom; I cannot describe my relief. She answered with the words I wanted to hear.
"Good for you", I responded.

A short glorious moment I thought ...she had slain the Dragon... without me. I was proud of her efforts and felt invigorated.

I almost wanted her to despise him as much as I did. I saw him as the enemy, not a comrade.

TWENTY- ONE

7th January - Day 172

The Dragon lives

On the way to work I told her how important it was for us to rebuild trust and confidence in each other. She agreed. I said I wanted the coming weekend to be all about us. I wanted her to stay with me all weekend. I wanted us to live as a couple and focus on each other with no interference from the outside world. She said that sounded wonderful and she was so looking forward to it. For the first time in weeks I relaxed. I looked at her and thought, what a beautiful girl; maybe I am still in love with you after all.

7 January

> Finished work Xoxo
> 5.52pm

> What have u got on tonight??
> Xxx
> 5.55pm

> A few domestic duties, and Skyping a friend back home.
> ♡ 5.59pm

> Would u like to go for a walk?
> Xxx
> 6.03pm

> Please don't be offended or upset, but I'd like to just have some me time tonight darling...
> 6.05pm

Sure!! I understand. Let's talk tomorrow. Xxx
6.06pm

Can I be frank with you baby? This has been on my mind a bit. When I think about moving in with you, I think about me losing my 'space'. let's talk when we see each other tomorrow. Are we having dinner tomorrow?
6.08pm

Yes, do u mean how do u have your Simone time if u r here??
Xxx
6.11pm

Yes that's what I mean. No offence about your place, but there's no real space for me if I need 'me time'. My friend, Peta, mentioned it, and now its swamping me. I'm sure it's not as big a problem as it seems to be in my head right now. I'll call you later. Love you xoxox
6.25pm

Yes Please !!!xoxo
6.28pm

8 January

Morning ♡ how did you sleep? I can't wait to see you tonight.
Love you ♡
6.39am

Good morning!! Yes slept like a rock!! Yes I can't wait too!! R we having sweets???
6.43am

Thought we were trying to lose weight???? lol.. xoxo
6.47am

I wasn't thinking of those sweets!! I'm thinking about making love to u!!
6.49am

Well, I didn't take any sleep over gear this morning... We will figure something out. Xxx
6.50am

Heheheheh!!! I am hungry for u!!!! We need to buy some oil!!!!
Xoxoxo
6.51pm

After dinner I will possibly head back home sweetheart. I still feel a little drained and not quite up to full strength.
7.01am

So a quiet night? U and your thoughts?? Xoxox
7.19am

Yes, just me and my thoughts Xo
7.20am

Well u need Simone time, we have been through the eye of a storm, and we made it!! I just feel so close to u, and love u deeply xoxoxo
7.33am

I love you too Michael!!!! I am petrified at some stage that I'll freak out on you again and have a panic attack at some point!!!!!
8.10am

Well let's talk about it and work out the answers. This is also about u growing up and growing as a person. U r transitioning, 35 is the beginning of your journey into a mature woman Physically, emotionally and sexually, and I want to be there to help u find yourself!!!! Especially sexually!!!! Bet you're smiling!!! ♡ ♡ ♡
8.18am

lol...yes I am ♡
8.18am

I remember as Friday moved forward and the hours melted before the weekend began, I had a luxurious feeling come over me. I felt alive and re-energised at the prospect of an amazing weekend. We could put the pieces back together. We could talk and laugh the way we used to.

10 January

Morning!! What a wonderful day. This is going to be a super weekend. I just have this feeling. I love you!!! ♡♡♡
7.21am

Good morning!!! I changed my alarm time and slept with the dark blinkers you bought for me and I have to say I feel much better!! Yes it will be an amazing weekend. I have so much love for u and I can't wait to make love to u!!!! u mean the world to me !! ♡♡♡
We will need to go grocery shopping... And dance in the aisles !!
Xoxo r u up for that ?? Xxx
7.29am

I am so glad you finally had a good sleep. It's so important to me when you are happy and healthy. you are my everything, and that is an amazing feeling....xoxox
7.32am

Do you want to go directly to the restaurant? or home? I don't mind either way.
7.33am

Sure let's discuss on the ferry?? What time will u finish?? Xoxo
7.35am

Close to half past 5
7.35am

There is a 5.27 ferry, otherwise
we have to wait till 6.30 ... I will
ring u at 3 xoxox
7.37am

Sounds great. could you grab me
a ticket, and I'll run straight
down. Ok xoxoxo
Thanks!! ♡
7.40am

Sure meet u at wharf 4
at 5.20!! Xxx
7.41am

But I also felt the fragility of my euphoria. I have never claimed to
have had any sixth sense but I remembered all too easily how in the
past my sense of well-being had been shocked and shattered by a
text or a phone call or some form of disturbance to our perfect
world. So when the text arrived at 4.35 pm on that Friday afternoon,
just as I was packing up my desk and about to walk out the door
towards the ferry wharf, I read it in disbelief...

Ok! ... This may or may not upset
you, and I'm hoping for the
latter, but I agreed to quickly
look at a house for Marco
tomorrow. It is in Double Bay. I
would love if you wanted to
come too, maybe as part of a
walk to brekkie? Understand if
you don't though. I can quickly
do myself. xoxoo
4.35pm

As I started walking to the wharf to meet her as arranged earlier that
morning, I felt with every step I took a rage rise within me and grip
my entire body. It was an anger that even shocked me; I couldn't
believe her words. She just didn't get it. Was I overreacting? I tried to

settle down but the anger locked my jaw. She arrived at the ferry and saw me. My face must have said it all. She looked down and asked me how much was the ticket that I had bought?

"Six dollars" I spat out. She reached into her purse and gave me the money and then ran off.

I got on the ferry and sat there alone. This was not how I envisaged the beginning of our weekend. And once again, Marco had been the cause of our problems. It was a beautiful summer's afternoon and thankfully, being on the water in one of the world's most beautiful harbours, soon had a soothing effect on me, and I allowed the tension to gently dissipate with the ebb and flow of the tide against the side of the vessel, as it moved slowly through the

U say please don't be mad. No I am so hurt and disappointed. U told me this was going to be our weekend. We were going to focus entirely on each other. We needed to nurture each other because it has been the worst week for us. U set the expectation when U agreed that u were not going to look at property for him. I feel so let down and I just was choking at the wharf. I was shocked into silence. I am sorry for that. I am also very sensitive right now, as I am sure u r too. I would like to make this weekend about us, but I can't force this if u don't want it. Clearly Marco is an ongoing element in your life for which I would like to support . But this is impossible when I have no direct relationship with him. I want to be in your life. All of it! And to support everything that u want . I still want this weekend to be special. Please call me. x
6.03pm

water taking me home.

I need to let off steam, so I'm going for a run. I will talk to you when I get back. I completely get where you are coming from. I want to work towards having something similar to you and your ex-wife's relationship. He has been a massive part of my life, and I guess I'm realising he will remain a massive part of my life in the future. I want you to meet, and one day you will, but now is not the right time. xoxo
6.10pm

It seems we have mixed communication here. I thought this weekend was about us. Yes agree we could view houses sometime. But as I understood it, this weekend wouldn't involve anything but us nurturing each other. As you started your original message with "don't be mad" you knew I wouldn't be over the moon and especially considering recent events, I hope you wouldn't want to make me "mad" when all I want to do is love and support you. Enjoy your run. Hear from you when you call. It's true I want our lives to be easy. But where they can't be easy I need us to be the priority and from that place it's easier to support one another with difficulties in our lives. Xxx
6.15pm

For the first time since Christmas, I contemplated what I had feared the most that we were in a terminal wind down. I couldn't believe it, but I thought to hell with her! I felt myself becoming consumed with anger. I couldn't believe how insensitive she had been. She had promised me she was going to tell him to look for his own place to live. She knew the damage she had caused over Christmas through her actions and choices. How stupid was this girl I asked myself? Did I really deserve this? And perhaps, for the first time, I questioned my own intelligence. Perhaps indeed I was the stupid one.

Later into the evening, I had cooled off and the inevitable text arrived. She pleaded with me, acknowledging her insensitivity and started to repeat the theme I had noted with dismay over Christmas. It was the 'you are far too good for me' line. 'I think it would be better for you to find someone who is worthy of you'. These texts infuriated me.

> Michael, I can't do this. I'm sorry. This is getting too hard. It shouldn't be this hard. I feel so much pressure to be something or someone to you, and right now, I don't know who I am. I fell in love way too quickly after my break up.
> I need now, more than ever, to be alone.
> Let me go. I will continue to hurt you, it seems to be a part of my makeup. You deserve better. Broke my heart seeing you so upset at the ferry. And I continue to hurt you...unintentionally, but it's still happening.
> 6:35 pm

Take as long as you like. When you are ready to love, come find me, I hope I have not got over you when you do. In the meantime I will hope to hear from you know I love you I want us to work, but only when you're ready to be partners in life and enjoy our love. X
6.40pm

She didn't want to talk and asked to be left alone. I was perfectly willing to make the cut there and then. I was descending into the abyss. "Cut now", I thought "...and save yourself a lot of pain." I would have walked but she texted again.

You need to know that I love you!
6.46pm

Why don't u pick up I want to talk to u??
6.47pm

Can u please call me?
6.48pm

Please don't come over today, I mean it! I want to be alone!!
6.59pm

Ok ...
7.00pm

Somewhere out there is your princess waiting to be swept off her feet. I'm not the one.
I have no doubt that you will find the person who will treat you in the way in which you deserve to be treated. We have gone

beyond repair. If I could twitch
my nose and undo all my
mistakes, I would do it in an
instant, but I am mortal, and so
the mistakes remain like large
thorns, sticking in our hearts.
I am so sorry!!!!
7.10pm

R u home?
7.11pm

She always had to have the last word and there was always a hook... I don't know why but I couldn't break the spell that she had cast over me. I changed and walked towards her apartment. My mind was racing over the words that I wanted to say to her. I rehearsed my speech with every step. I turned towards her building and noticed a figure coming towards me carrying shopping bags. It was her. She had been for a run as she had explained and obviously gone shopping to buy some groceries.

For the first time since I had known her, she cast a withering glance at me. She said nothing.

"Let me take those bags" I said, and I took the shopping bags in my hand. We went up to her apartment. The next two hours I endured a seesaw of emotion. One minute she hardened herself and pleaded for us to end the relationship. The next minute she was in my arms sobbing and telling me how much she loved me. When she returned to this proclamation of love, I decided to bid my farewell. I urged her to think about what I had said overnight and we'd talk tomorrow. I remember walking back home...it was dark and I was thinking... what a great start to the weekend that was supposed to have been so special.

I thought about what Rhett Butler said in that literary classic... "Tomorrow is another day!" Despite this, as I walked through Rushcutters Bay Park and heard the gentle rustle of the breeze through the trees, I also felt my love for her was disappearing, being carried away by the breeze; it was "gone with the wind", so to speak.

TWENTY-TWO

11th January - Day 176

Lost...

11 January

Morning... After our talk last night, I have decided that I'm going to get some help through a psychologist.
It's obvious my issues run deeply, and I'm not equipped on my own to deal with them. I am hurting you, and pushing you away, which is the opposite of what I want. it doesn't make sense, and I now know, that
I really need help. I don't want to lose you. But I will if I don't attend to this NOW!! Take care of yourself!
10.06am

Can u please call?
10.16am

Where r u?
10.19am

This is the first step to u getting well. Please don't push me away.
Xx
10.24am

I am not angry with u xx
10.28am

I have tried to call but no answer. I wanted to say how your text made me feel. So proud of u! I want u to know that I know it must be hell to come to terms with these issues . U have taken the first step. Please don't push me away. I stand with u, through good and bad. I thought u didn't care last night, so I want to take u out for a snack tonight. Just us and the sunset
How about it ? Pick u Up at 7. Xxx
11.20am

I love u very much ...
We can beat this together !!
Xoxo
11.37am

I'm on the bus rereading your texts. I could cry. I love you so much. I'm trying to let you go, but I don't want to, and I can't. And you're fighting for me, and that just speaks volumes. You never left my heart, I hope you know that!
I'll see you at 7pm ♡
11:40 am

Yes, I never give up on things I believe in, and I believe in u and us... ♡ ♡ ♡
11.42am

Once again I felt bruised by this exchange, on Saturday morning I brooded and my mind wandered for what seemed like hours. I made arrangements to see her on Saturday night and I thought a return to one of our favourite venues might augur well. It was a small cafe off Macleay Street in Potts Point. We had gone there many times and certainly in happier times. It was intimate and fun and the food was great.

As I prepared to walk to her apartment, I had a sense of foreboding as to our future together. I thought about all those amazing moments that we had shared only weeks before. And I thought if I could turn the conversation over dinner to how we had been; it might just jolt her back to a realisation that what we did indeed have was very special.

So over dinner, I deliberately reminisced and talked about how I met that beautiful young girl at the Crystal bar, on tango night. We talked about our Skyping and the desperate urgency that gripped us both once we realised we had met that special person.

I remembered how concerned I was to learn that Marco had turned up in Tahiti to ambush her. I confessed to her that I was one phone call away from booking a ticket to come over and rescue her. Her eyes lit up and she giggled with delight. We seemed to capture some of the magic. I talked endlessly about our five days in Sydney. I reminded her of some of the beautiful memories that we had created together; the walks to the Art Gallery, the bookshops and the evening at the Opera. I looked into her eyes and told her how she had made me feel when we first made love. Her eyes welled with tears and she gripped me by the hand with the desperate urgency of someone falling.

Dinner passed and we taxied back to my apartment. Our evening ritual began. I would simply undress, brush my teeth and get into bed. I lit candles; and put on music that soothed and molded the

191

atmosphere. She would emerge from the bathroom in her black slip, and slide into bed with me.

Our lovemaking was gentle, our connection profound, and we held each other for hours, talking and rebuilding the bond that I was so certain had been shattered. In the morning I lay awake genuinely confused. She snoozed next to me and I watched her sleep. She had never had trouble sleeping unlike myself. I would toss and turn and ultimately take a handful of herbal sleeping tablets to assist in dozing off. When she opened her eyes I was looking at her. Her beautiful glance back melted my doubts and I just wanted to be inside her warm and rested body. I kissed her gently while my hands started to explore her every curve. She surrendered to my touch, closed her eyes and smiled as I gently parted her legs. Our morning sex was as amazing as ever. Her wetness drove me crazy. I kissed her neck as I gently pulsated in and out of her. Her eyes still closed; the smile on her face said it all. She whispered, "take me" and I knew she was close to cumming. I wanted to climax with her, I wanted to feel her tightness and the quivering of her orgasm with mine. She started to kiss me deeply, our breath was in perfect rhythm. I exploded into her and she let out her beautiful deep groan as she bit me gently on my lip.

It felt amazing. I tenderly kissed her shoulder and we fell into a deep sleep entwined together in the morning sun.

When I woke I was torn and conflicted. The angel had returned to my life. Last night there had been no mention of Marco, no phone calls or texts and this morning was incredible. It was just the two of us. It was perfect. But it had been perfect before, and she had lapsed. Was I being too hard on her? Was I the control freak? I was debating this in my mind trying to work out the answer. Was there an answer? Could I trust her? Whilst these thoughts danced around in my mind, she stirred awake from our morning lovemaking slumber and looked up at me and smiled.

"Good morning" I said, kissing her gently again on her bare shoulder.

"Good morning" she replied smiling as she stretched.

She was like a contented cat that had just had an afternoon sleep in the sun. She was all doe eyed. Her smell drove me crazy. I wanted every part of her again. I slid down and parted her thighs gently.

The doubt and uncertainty which had been swirling around in my mind disappeared and we spent Sunday together, but not before exploring each other over and over again. Our love making seemed to have an innocent almost sublime quality.

There is something quite decadent about a lazy Sunday morning with a lover; the preparation of a savoury breakfast, the aromas of toast and fresh coffee, reclining on the sofa together reading newspapers, chatting, and simply enjoying the presence of each other.

I said good night to her that evening and slept the sleep of someone exhausted. Not only through physical exertion but through the exasperation and frustration of not knowing whether I could return to the position of absolute trust and confidence. Saturday and Sunday had been wonderful. All I could do was try to accept her words and beautiful texts.

On Monday morning the sun shone and the world appeared perfect again.

TWENTY–THREE

12th January - Day 177

Dinner

We had agreed to meet regularly midweek for dinner. We called it our "date night". There has even been a movie dedicated to that theme and it seemed like fun. We would try and pick a new restaurant or café and explore the menus and talk about our day at work. We talked about our friends and their issues. It was comforting to know we now seemed rock solid in our commitment and relationship as we discussed some of the traumas our friends were enduring with their relationships.

Simone talked again about her Singapore work conference with great excitement. I'd actually forgotten about it and asked more about the detail. I didn't think twice about it.

I had planned a surprise and decided it was appropriate to tell her that night.

"Guess what?" She looked up eagerly, "we are going away for the weekend. Not this weekend, but next."

"Where?" She asked. I didn't answer straight away. I was grinning at her and enjoying the slow, teasing, revelation of my romantic gesture. But part of me was also scrutinising her reaction. It was as though I was now on the lookout for any tell-tale signs of her obsession with Marco.

"Where?" she repeated. "The Blue Mountains", I said.

She said she couldn't wait and this was a wonderful, wonderful surprise. Later I texted the details of my thoughts.

12 January

> I want to book a couple of days for us on the Australia Day weekend Sat / Sunday night Up the mountains. Just us. Just romance and relaxing R u ok with the dates?! Xxx
> 5.17pm

Our first romantic holiday together.
Well....apart from Singapore.
That was pretty romantic. Ohhhh
I love you so much!! ♡
5.19pm

> Great I will try and make the booking xxx
> 5.25pm

I would like to contribute to things financially, including this trip away. I have to wait till next pay though, as I fixed my mums car when I went back, and that took a lot of my savings....sorry

that's actually really embarrassing for me to tell you.
5.35pm

> Sure ... Don't worry so much about that side of things!! They have a beautiful restaurant called Darleys. I know u won't eat a lot but at least one course and we share a sweet !!! Xoxo
> 5.40pm

What is Darleys? ♡ ♡ ♡
5.40pm

Darley's is the signature restaurant at Lillianfels in Katoomba. It is simply stunning. I might even have a glass of wine!! Xoxox
5.42pm

Sounds great. u know I don't eat much, but I will definitely try something on the menu. Fine dining serves suit my small appetite...lol I think a glass of wine is apt, as we discuss our future together. xoxo
5.45pm

I wanted to go the whole month without drinking but I will join u in a toast to us!!!
5.46pm

Hey, that is completely up to you. Don't let me interfere with your detox commitment. The sentiment will be there regardless Xoxo
5.49pm

No it's ok ... One glass is neither here nor there!!! Xoxox all
5.50pm

All booked!!! 3 course dinner at Darleys! It will be a Wonderful night!! Xxx
6.15pm.

I just got butterflies. The excitement of being alone on a beautiful romantic escape.
Xoxoxo
6.18pm

Yes!!! It will be amazing!! google Lillianfels Xxx
6.19pm

Sweet dreams my prince. I wish you were beside me right now. I'm wondering if we should start considering the "trial" moving in soon? I think we are ready to move to the next step. I go to sleep with a heart full of love and absolute happiness. We have a great future to look forward to. Your love and commitment is unwavering, and that gives me such strength and hope
♡♡♡ 9.32pm

The trip to the mountains was two weeks away, so once again I suggested a quiet weekend and she agreed that would be fun. Just us building upon what we had achieved on the last weekend. No more issues to deal with. I think she understood my feelings in relation to Marco and I hoped she might finally understand my sensitivity.

17 January

Marco has rung and needs me to look at a place tomorrow. I'm asking you for your thoughts? I was only going to if I had time. Otherwise not! Love you! Xoxo
7.14pm

Hello??? I'm asking for your opinion. Please don't ignore me, or be mad with me. If you say no, then
I won't go. YOU are first and foremost my priority!!! you are the one I love ok? ♡
7.28pm

Thank u so much!!! I think that we need to be together, and concentrate on us !!! U r the woman I love too!!!
7.38pm

Agree! ♡ ♡
7.38pm

The days passed as they always do and once again the weekend arrived. We agreed to meet on Saturday at lunch this time.

18 January

Do u want to cook some dinner tonight? Or would u like to go out?! I am entirely easy. Just want to kiss u a lot! I have almond oil!! ♡ ♡
8.03am

You make me laugh. I think cooking sounds fab.
8.04am

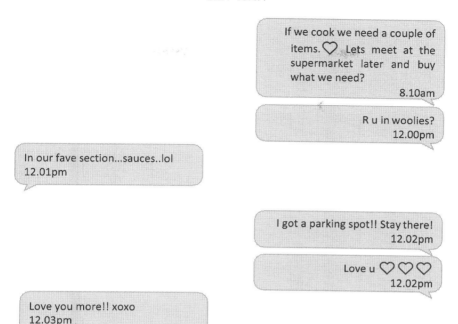

If we cook we need a couple of items. ♡ Lets meet at the supermarket later and buy what we need?
8.10am

R u in woolies?
12.00pm

In our fave section...sauces..lol
12.01pm

I got a parking spot!! Stay there!
12.02pm

Love u ♡ ♡ ♡
12.02pm

Love you more!! xoxo
12.03pm

One of the things that we had done on weekends in preparation for our cooking adventures was to go to the local grocery specialist and buy our provisions. We had done this many times prior to Christmas and it was simple good fun. We both enjoyed looking at the produce and working out what we needed to fulfill the recipe that we were attempting to cook that evening. Before long we were pushing a shopping trolley down our favourite aisle and plucking items from the shelves and stocking up on ingredients and other foods, fruits, vegetables and spices.

By the time we headed home we decided that we would go for a swim in the pool before we started to cook. We were not talking much but there was silent understanding between us. I only had to look into her eyes and I could see what she was thinking. It was extraordinary and generally, I was about 95 percent accurate.

I suggested that it was time to start cooking and so we went upstairs and started preparing the ingredients. Once again I relaxed and thought that this was going to be a beautiful evening. What could go wrong? The mere fact that I even thought about something occurring which might ruin our evening unsettled me. And as if it were again a premonition to reality it turned out to be just around the corner, yet again.

I was throwing some onion into the pan and suddenly her phone rang. I winced. I looked over to the bench where her phone lay and yes, guess who? It was Marco, of course. She looked at the phone and looked at me. I tried to be nonchalant. We continued to cook over the pan as the phone rang out. I thought to myself, well maybe she might let this go and demonstrate that she could focus on me, and us, without interruption. But as I turned to walk to the sink she moved over to the bench, took her phone, looked at me and said, "I have to call him back."

She took the phone and walked out of the room and dialed. Once again I had that terrible sinking feeling and knew again she was crossing the line. They spoke in Italian for a few minutes and then she said goodbye.

The food was almost cooked and the final preparations were undertaken in silence. She could sense I was deeply dissatisfied. I started the conversation over dinner. I said I couldn't believe that after all the arguments that she could still not understand that interrupting our time, while we were cooking, to specially phone him back was so disrespectful. I know that normally I wouldn't be so precious about this. I just really didn't want him to have any part of her new life.

She tried to defend herself saying that it was only a short conversation. I asked her what was so important that she had to ring back. She looked down and said he wanted to tell her about his latest bungee jump! Talk about hitting a raw nerve.

I couldn't believe it – bungee jumping again! What is it about jumping off a cliff with a huge rubber band tied around your feet?

Did I give a damn? Not at all, but it had ruined the beautiful atmosphere that we were creating. Shot... Gone... And she knew it. So without finishing her meal she got up and went to the bedroom for a few minutes. She came back with her things in her bag and said she wanted to go home.

"You are free to go and you are free to come. It's your decision", I said coldly. I walked to the door, opened it and said "goodbye." When the door closed my isolation suffocated me. Had I been too harsh? Had I overreacted?

But I was beginning to really understand the pattern that was re-emerging with her conduct.

I thought to myself, if I have got it right there will be a text within an hour or so with an apology or an explanation, and then there would be the forgiveness. And sure enough about an hour later the text arrived.

18 January

Why can you not believe that I am completely over my ex, and it is you that I love? Did I do the wrong thing by answering my phone? possibly...
But I don't think the punishment fits the crime. I don't want to lose you.
I want to marry you!!!! one day!!!! can we talk???
9.38pm

Simone of course we can talk. I wanted to talk tonight, but u left
Let's talk tomorrow?
Get some rest
9.44pm

I'd like to come over now if you don't mind?
9.46pm

> Of course! Catch a taxi,
> I want to make love to u.
> 9.48pm

In half an hour we were both lying in each other's arms in bed as though nothing had happened, but the reality was, it had happened again, and it hurt. I needed a shower to gather my thoughts. I wanted to wash away everything that was encroaching on my future with this beautiful woman and feel the purity of the love we had created once again. I was lost in my thoughts under the cleansing hot steamy water when she walked into the bathroom and opened the shower door. Her naked image melted me, I put out my hand to guide her into the shower.

Together we held each other, the water hiding the tears I wanted to shed, skin to skin, just holding one another.

I needed be inside her and her beautiful erect nipples told me she was feeling the same intimacy and joy that came when we were in our own world. I lifted her up and slid effortlessly inside of her, gently pushing her body against the tiles, her legs wrapped around my hips. I made love to her slowly and passionately under the purity of the water that soaked our bodies, sucking her nipples while she held her arms around my neck. Letting go of her inhibitions she gave herself to me. It was surreal, gentle, passionate and erotic. We came together with a gentle whimper, gripping each other tightly, but something was missing for me. I dried her body in silence.

She fell asleep after our steamy lovemaking, but I couldn't. My mind was wondering again. I was traversing familiar territory. I had thought the same thoughts before, and was thinking them again. What was going on? Was she really over him? Was he really over her? I thought it all very childish, but it occupied my mind like a fever gripping me, not letting go.

Sunday thankfully turned out to be a wonderful day. We went for walks and talked and laughed just the way we used to. We even looked at her iPad photos, some of which included Marco.

19 January

Looking at the photos with you made me realize how much I love you.
12.50pm

Another amazing day to add to all the others we have experienced together.
I guess I realized that I have some patterns of behaviour that I need to address, like jumping every time Marco clicks his fingers.
I don't want to harp on about it, but I guess recognizing it, makes it easier to fix. I'm glad I had the guts to ask to come back last night, and I'm glad you said I could. Our love is strong, and that makes our difficult discussions easier to face. What are your thoughts? Night my darling.....Sitting watching a movie, missing you so much. So I told Marco tonight that I won't always be available or on call to take his calls, and not to panic and call me continuously until he gets on to me. He gets it and completely understands. He said he would like to meet you when he gets back. I'm excited to start our life together. Have to say I do feel quite vulnerable, because I feel my love for you is so strong, that you control my heart strings.
But I trust you more than I have anyone, and know that you will take care of me. Some people

look forever to find their soul mate, and are not always successful. The universe has given you to me, and I am eternally grateful. You are the "ONE". I love you ♡
10:00 pm

Good night...! ♡
10.01pm

20 January

Good morning!! I just woke up. I will work from home. Just read your messages, they r very moving. I understand how u feel about feeling vulnerable, I feel a little of it myself. Let's work together to rebuild love and trust And our team spirit!!! I love u. ♡
7.23am

Team Michael and Simone. I like it!!!!...No..I LOVE IT!!!! ♡♡
7.28am

TWENTY- FOUR

20th January - Day 185

The iPad

I was now turning our discussion towards the special weekend that I had planned in the Blue Mountains. She was so excited and it thrilled me to see her joy. As I explained to her, we were going to stay at one of my favourite hotels... Lilianfels. It's an old-world hotel that shares the family estate of one of our first Chief Justices, and the signature restaurant, Darley's, now carries his name.

I thought to myself that this weekend away would really test my feelings towards her. If I couldn't regain my trust and confidence after a weekend in the mountains then I knew I had lost her.

As I had said, that weekend she had brought over her iPad. She had wanted to show me some family photographs that were stored in its memory. After she had left on Sunday evening I looked over towards the couch and realised that she had left the iPad at my place.

I picked it up and opened the flap and the device came to life. No password. There before me were all the applications able to be opened by anyone. I was gripped by a sense of wickedness with the thought of opening her emails and texts. Should I? Would I like her looking at my texts? I had nothing to hide. I agonised for minutes with my finger hovering above the email icon. I pressed it... and the page configured her emails.

I remember that she had told me she had transferred her account to her new laptop, but this iPad still had some 30 plus e-mails which spanned October, November and December of the previous year. I counted 26 between her and Marco. My heart sank. I quickly looked at her Skype records and texts. Once again there was evidence of heavy traffic between the two of them over this period. And these were the months when we were madly 'in love' with each other!

She had told me even when she was living in Singapore months before, that she had explained to Marco how we had met and how we were now seeing each other. She told me that he knew about my Singapore visit and that everything was in her words... 'Cool'. So why was there so much intense communication? What were the messages? Dare I open one of the e-mails and read their contents? Was I over-reacting?

The answer came within seconds as I pressed the button. Damn! They are all in Italian; colloquial Italian at that. No match for my high school basics. So I rang a friend of mine who spoke the language fluently. Peter was a willing accomplice to assist in the translation.

On Monday evening I walked to his house with her iPad under my arm; the evidence. I felt like the proverbial thief in the night. Or a spy who had to decrypt the intercepted enemy dispatch. I felt dirty. Distrust of her trapped me and seeped through my consciousness.

Upon arrival we set about our task of opening each communication and understanding its contents. My apprehension started to diminish with the relatively banal nature of each communication. But two things hit me, one of which was to give me a clue to the whole predicament. Firstly the level of familiarity in the way they greeted each other was inconsistent with the fact they'd broken up as a couple. Italian is a funny language Peter told me.

"It doesn't necessarily mean that they are intimate but these terms they are using, definitely reflect affection". She would call him "Baby" and in response he would call her... "Beautiful".

But the real clue to cracking the case appeared in an email that was sent on 19 October. She complained to him that she had to go to a Chinese wedding. I checked my diary and confirmed that was the date that we had gone to my colleague's wedding. She had gone as my partner, my girlfriend, whatever. My colleague was actually Korean but the reception took place in a Chinese restaurant. Her email to… "baby" … complained that she didn't really want to go but, couldn't get out of it because it was a "colleague from work". A "colleague from work"! Was I the "colleague from work"?!

I had been demoted from 'boyfriend' to 'colleague'!

We both sat there in silence. Peter looked at me and I looked down.

My brain refused to accept the possibility that was suddenly so crystal clear. She had NOT told him about me. In all the emails that we deciphered, there was not one reference to her new, exciting, magnificent, wonderful boyfriend or her life in Sydney with me.

This correspondence was evidence that their relationship was continuing as if nothing had happened between them. It just didn't make sense. I thanked Peter for his help and walked home carrying the iPad and my torn emotions.

TWENTY- FIVE

22nd January - Day 187

Lilianfels

My mind started to deconstruct and analyse what had been happening over the last few weeks. A lawyer's instinct gripped me – evidence and the forensic assembly of facts. Propositions for and propositions against. Certainly, the events over Christmas now took on an entirely different meaning. Was I dealing with a monstrous liar? I just could not get my head around this being a possibility; surely not my delicate Simone. But it just didn't make sense. Perhaps it did and I couldn't process it. Or I simply refused to allow myself to believe the possibility that this was, in fact, the cold hard reality.

When I got home I opened the iPad again and this time took a journey through some of her albums. There were hundreds of photographs of her and Marco, she had kept them in various different albums and they were easily recognisable by reference to holidays. I looked at them bemused yet detached. I knew she had every right to store photographs of another time and these were taken years before we had met. So I viewed them without a sense of resentment or jealousy. It seemed to me that there were very few photographs of the two of them which expressed real joy or happiness. This was the strange thing when they were together and photographed. She bore a sadness in her eyes that was self-evident to me. He looked happy enough but there was always a sense of weariness in her expression. I could read her eyes; it seemed that was my special talent with Simone.

I saw the photographs of her family and especially those taken at her Uncle's funeral. It took me a number of hours to look at them all. I put down the iPad and stared into space. I felt as though I had trespassed, but I felt justified.

Something was terribly wrong and I was determined to get to the bottom of it before it destroyed me. The Wednesday night before we were to leave for the mountains she stayed with me. I watched her every time she opened her iPhone and memorised each digit as she applied her entry code. She did it very quickly and often tried to turn away. I was patient, I was hunting the prey. I was not at all comfortable taking her phone and testing the codes whilst she was in the shower. I knew ultimately that if it had come to this, then we were finished. I felt horrible but determined.

I tried a number of combinations and on my third attempt the phone sprang to life. I knew the code now and looked at her emails. One after the other: Marco to her and her to Marco. I scrolled down. There were even photographs of apartments and properties. She had indeed been looking at properties for him despite her assurances to me. I heard the shower water cease, so I put down the phone, clicking it off.

The following few days continued with us exchanging the same kind of texts that had been prevalent throughout our relationship, but I felt like an imposter. Part of me was trying to ignore my newly gained 'intel'; another part wanted to immerse into a covert operation to get to the bottom of this. In order to do this, I had to continue on as though I knew or suspected nothing. It was one of the toughest things I have ever endured.

As a distraction I had invited my daughter to come over for dinner the Thursday before we went away. It was a nice change of pace.

22 January

> Have a wonderful dinner with Naomi, and say hi from me please! I'm still plodding away at work. ♡
> 5.55pm

> Yes I will xxx
> 6.00pm

> That was very short...lol
> I get you're still a little wary.
> It's understandable.
> 6.08pm

I ignored the comment.

> We had a great dinner. I made puttanesca and it was delicious. Naomi says 'Hi.' How was work today?? Xoxox
> 8.56pm

> Only finished 10 mins ago. Long day. Hope dinner was yummy. Feel like talking? Xo
> 8.58pm

> When u get home Skype?
> 9.00pm

Can you tell me honestly???
Do you still love the idea of me moving in? or do you have reservations? I'm stressing out a little. I was thinking, I will need to give notice here.
9.46pm

I understand, let's talk tomorrow. I don't want u to stress. I think we will work through everything ♡
9.51pm

Thank you. I love you!
9.52pm

Yes and I love u and I want to make love to u ♡
9.54pm

mmmm me too. I love falling asleep afterwards, all snuggled together. waking up with you spooning me. I feel so protected and secure when I wake up like that. ♡
9.56pm

Good u r getting better at it !!
I want u to let yourself go on the weekend, don't hold back.xxx
9.59pm

I will give it a red hot go...lol love you....night....
I'll sleep on the rent issue.
♡ ♡ ♡
10.02pm

> Good night sleep tight ♡ ♡ ♡
> 10.04pm

23 January

Morning! Can't wait till dinner tonight
I love you!! ♡ ♡ ♡
7.17am

> Good morning! Slept well!! Went for a run!! Yes I am looking forward to dinner too !! I missed u last night, missed u next to me!
> Xoxoxo
> 7.26am

seems I'm always missing you lately...
What have you done to me? lol
Hope we have a great weekend. ♡ ♡
7.27am

> Yes ... Don't hope.. Make it the best !!! U and I need it!!
> Xoxo ♡ ♡
> 7.29am

We most certainly do!! it will be brilliant!!!
7.29am

> That's the spirit!!! I need u and your love ... And without any distractions ...xoxo
> 7.31am

We were due to leave on Saturday morning and it was about an hour and a half drive to our destination.

25 January

> Good morning!!! Xoxox
> Just finished my run to Double
> Bay. Having food, finishing
> packing and then picking up my
> baby !!! Xoxoxo ♡ ♡ ♡ ♡
> 8.08am

I've been running. The city is sparkling. See you soon xoxo
8.10am

I'm sure I'll survive your car.
10.46am

> On my way!!! Car is dirty!!
> Sorry ... Xoxox
> 10.45am

> I am early, as usual.
> Ready when u r ...xoxox
> 10.48am

I drove over to pick her up and she was genuinely excited and happy. I suddenly realised for the very first time that I was acting out a role now and not really being myself. I forced myself to engage in conversation almost to the point of submitting to another personality. I kept repeating to myself 'Don't lose it... Don't lose it... get to the bottom of this, and then you will know.'

On the trip up to the mountains she raised the Singapore conference again. I admitted to her that I hadn't really taken it in when she had discussed it before, and asked her to tell me about it so that I could make suggestions to assist her in the marketing role that she had been asked to fulfill. But my questions, while feigning interest, served a dual purpose: I was probing her.

"You know I have been to probably 50 of these types of conferences in my career? I have manned trade booths and delivered presentations, I know exactly what goes on at these events." Stopped at a red light, I stared deeply into her eyes when I made these comments looking for a flinch. And I could see it as though she lost focus and slightly turned her eyes from me.

We arrived at Leura village just 20 minutes from our final destination. We went for a walk, looked at the shops and had a small snack. This was the same village we had visited when she first came to Sydney from Tahiti. It had real significance for us. We had found a furniture shop and had made comments about the beautiful stock on display. We had looked at each other then and said, "Are you thinking what I'm thinking?" And the answer was obviously "Yes". We were thinking about what it would be like to live together and make a home with this sort of furniture. I joked about the same comment when we went to the shop again, but this time my words were hollow and I was acting. So, we drove on to our destination and checked in at the hotel. She asked me sheepishly how many girls I had brought to this hotel. I looked at her and grinned.

"What sort of question is that? A gentleman never discusses these things!" I said grinning. I then got quite serious and looked her in the eyes:

"I'm not going to lie; you know I would never lie to you." I said. I detected a weakness in her expression; almost guilt. I passed over it quickly and said:

"Yes, I have been here with a few people but never with anyone who has meant as much to me as you do right now. I hope you believe me?"

"Yes." She said meekly. It was all she could muster.

We went down to the main lounge and after ordering some tea, sat chatting. It was so old world; full of cosy deep seated Chesterfields. I was feeling quite relaxed considering I was waiting to pounce at any given opportunity to look at her phone. Then right on cue she excused herself and retreated to the bathroom. She had left her phone in front of her on the table. I knew I had about thirty seconds, and with precision timing, I quickly entered the code. Sure-enough there they were: emails from you know who! With my phone I took pictures of the most recent e-mails and quickly put her phone back. I felt exhilaration at how quickly and efficiently I had performed this task, but also sickened that at my age, I was behaving in such a despicable manner, unnatural for me. I thought to myself, "How could I do this?"

I was at war with myself.

She came back smiling and I said,

"You've inspired me I'd better go too!" and off I went to the bathroom. As I was walking, I was thinking that even James Bond would have been proud of these moves, but I was suddenly saddened to think that my love life had been reduced not to an exciting Bond story, but to a cheap spy novel...and not so cheap at this hotel!

I felt intense relief not at the prospect of going to the bathroom, but being in the small little cubicle behind closed, locked doors and in total privacy. I could look at the photographs I had just taken. Of course the messages were in Italian, but my Italian was good enough to understand their gist. She was telling him that she was off to the airport to fly to Hong Kong and that if her mother called could he please speak to her. He wished her a good weekend and hoped that it wouldn't be 'too stressful'. I walked back to the table looking at her as she smiled at me. But as I sat down my mind kept turning over the possibilities and meanings which could be attributed to these messages. Anyhow I soon learned one thing I was capable of and that was... a good performance. We chatted and soon realised that we needed to get ready for dinner. We went up to our room to prepare for our dinner at Darley's. I hoped she might even eat some food!

We quickly changed and went downstairs for a drink; the bar was full so I suggested we go to the billiard room. Another couple were playing pool and I suggested that we challenge them, and the winner had to buy drinks. I noticed that she felt uneasy and I turned to her and she said she had to go back to the room. I continued playing with the young couple and then looked at my phone, I'd received a text from her.

26 January

> Why do you feel the need to tell strangers our story? It's embarrassing.
> That's not the issue though. My first nightmare with my father's best friend was in my grand parents pool table room. Sorry ... I couldn't bare it....
> 6.51pm

She said she'd be down in ten minutes and I said I would meet her back in the lounge area.

Whenever she mentioned the issue of what had happened in the past my all-consuming suspicions were temporarily suspended. I wanted to protect her and nurture her and these instincts overwhelmed me. So off to dinner we went. She had worn one of her black cocktail dresses and looked beautiful.

We ate dinner, drank wine and once again were floating on the wings of romance and allowed ourselves to be swept up by the moment. We talked about how we had met and it did feel wonderful to be with her in this setting. I suspended reality for a few hours but knew that I was kidding myself. And kid myself I did because as we walked back to our room, the reality of those emails flew back into my mind. But I was so caught up with the moment and consumed with her beauty that I pushed my suspicions to the back of my mind.

Once inside the room I tingled with anticipation, as I pushed her against the wall and kissed her deeply and passionately. I thumbed her little black dress up to her lacy panties and slid my hand inside them, my finger slipping easily into her drenched warm pussy. I slid the delicate straps off her shoulders and the dress dropped to the floor. I love the feeling that comes when undressing a woman – a sense of anticipation, a sense of inevitability.

I dropped to my knees, my tongue ready to explore her wetness. I wanted to taste her; she parted her legs and let out a soft groan. This was her vulnerability and her body was trembling. I wanted to feel her orgasm as I explored her with my mouth. Her groans became more desperate and hungry. I knew she was ready. I kept my tongue flicking along her body, teasing her breasts and sucking her nipples as I made my way up to her lips. I pushed my hard cock inside her. She was wet and her groans were growing more guttural as she completely released herself to me. I pumped her against the wall and gripped her breasts. I was heaving, trying to gain air. I came hard.

I withdrew my cock from her and we collapsed onto each other, and we started laughing. We lay for a while in silence our chests heaving in protest for oxygen. My contentment was short lived as I remembered who this lady was and what had recently been revealed to me. At that moment I felt so utterly and completely alone.

"I think I will have a shower" she said. "Good idea!"

TWENTY-SIX

26th January - Day 191

Happy Australia Day

Prior to us leaving for our weekend, Simone had spoken about her desire to try abseiling and it had registered with me. The image of her standing on the bungee platform with Marco was something that I had struggled with for months. So I had secretly enquired as to whether we could go abseiling in the mountains.

The concierge had confirmed there was an abseiling company that worked locally and that we could join a group that was setting off that afternoon. I made the booking and kept it secret. When I told her after breakfast her eyes lit up with disbelief. Yes! I was a "real man" too, I thought. And then I thought how immature I really was. I had subconsciously submitted to a "pissing contest" with Marco and now it was my turn to show her that I could be a physical outdoorsman too!

So we set off to join the group and soon found ourselves standing on the side of a mountain cliff being instructed in the art of abseiling. It was a misty afternoon soon accompanied by rain and a cold wind. We started the afternoon's activity with a very small jump of five metres which seemed hardly terrifying. I thought to myself this is no big deal one simply lowered oneself over the side and let out the slack in the rope and in three steps I found myself back on terra firma. Piece of cake!

Little did I realise the next jump would be 15 metres of sheer vertical terror. We had to go straight over a real cliff and were hanging against the side of a mountain. When I went over the surge of adrenaline was electric. I had to summon every ounce of focus to control my panic and the ensuing image of myself plunging to my death. I couldn't believe my stupidity. I couldn't believe that I was doing this. But I did and after what seemed to be an eternity I eventually reached the ground.

Simone's turn came and she also baulked. The instructor had to talk her through it and calm her. She even asked me to move back so I wouldn't see her cry. Ultimately she went over the side and made it to the bottom. We then moved on to the 30 metre cliff. Something inside me snapped and before I knew what I was doing, I was backing away from the edge and started to dismantle my gear.

"Count me out, I'm not doing this", I blurted to the instructor.

He was quite friendly and assured in his response. "That's okay we don't push people if they don't want to do it". I knew I had the physical strength and the technique and they reassured me again that if I wanted to change my mind all I had to do was say so.

I sat back and watched all the others go over, including Simone, and then I thought to myself, I don't need to prove anything anymore, to anyone. I remembered then that I had another burden to carry that day; my private agony of the knowledge that she was lying to me.

She came back with the group after about half an hour. I don't know why, but I found it hard to disguise my foul mood. I didn't talk much in the car going back and she thought that she had upset me.

"No, I was upset with myself for not doing it" I told her I had only organised it, because I wanted her to see that I could do these sorts of things. Do the sort of things that she had done with Marco. She held my hand in the car tenderly as we went back to the hotel. In truth I knew that my mood was childish and not justified. I also knew that Marco had won the pissing contest, and sadly he wasn't even here or aware he was competing. Why was I continuing to compete with a young man almost 20 years my junior? What was I trying to prove? To who? The blackness of my mood seemed to smother me in the car. It was obvious to everyone, and only added fuel to my fire. I wanted to shout out.... 'I'm not the bad guy here... You guys have no idea what this lady has done to me'.... For God's sake, get a grip and snap out of it Michael!!!

We returned to our hotel and as we indulged in hot showers and got changed into warm clothes the weather improved a little, so we decided to go for a long walk. We looked through art galleries and re-energised at coffee houses, and even found a wine tasting. But alas, I was no longer feeling so enamored with her. I was seeing things through crystal clear glasses. The grey, overcast weather infected my mood. I felt that something had snapped inside my head. My whole attitude towards her had changed and everything was different. I don't think she could sense it.

We went back to the hotel and spent the afternoon having sex. It was funny, because the whole time I had known her, Simone had always expressed disinterest or disgust in giving or receiving oral. But on this occasion to warm up from our outing she took a quick shower then emerged from the bathroom wearing nothing. She was normally self-conscious of her flat chest and would usually cover up or dim the lights, but today she was completely uninhibited.

She sauntered over to me, staring deeply into my eyes, biting her lower lip with her hips swaying provocatively. For the first time ever she looked like a minx. She stopped in front of me and as she unbuttoned and unzipped my pants, she said in seductive whisper: "I want to thank you for the most amazing weekend" and then as she got down on her knees, she slid my jeans and underpants down. She certainly had my full attention. I forgot instantly any previous negative thoughts I had of her as she took me into her mouth. I let out a deep groan as my head went back and my hand was behind her head gently coercing her to go deeper and change the rhythm from slow and deep to quick short sharp sucks around the top of my

223

head. I could tell she wasn't well practiced, but this was the first time in eight or so months that I'd had head and it was fantastic. I was so engorged and was close to climaxing. I wanted her to experience my full explosion, to swallow my essence. I held her head close and felt her lips completely around my penis. She didn't resist, she moved her tongue around teasing me with every swirl; I came with a pulsating intensity that shocked me. I sat on the edge of the bed and looked at her. She smiled then pushed me back and slid herself on top of me and began to kiss me. After a few minutes, I was aroused again. I flicked her on her back and entered her immediately. Instead of our usual gentle love making, I was driven by a passion of frustration and confusion and hurt. I drove deep inside her. She didn't resist, her legs were wrapped around me and she had a slight smile on her face as she held my hips and encouraged me to go faster and deeper. She stared deeply into my eyes. Our orgasm reached a crescendo. We climaxed together and both released a primal scream.

We lay next to each other recovering, neither of us talking, just gently stroking each other. Soon the afternoon had turned into night, and we had fallen asleep in each other's arms.

We woke and indulged in a lazy breakfast. We were both ravenous and needed to restock the energy stores. After our leisurely breakfast we packed and by mid- morning were in the car heading home. I dropped her back to her place kissed her and we said our goodbyes.

By the time I had got home I had received a long and loving text from her. Her words moved me. She explained why she had fallen in love with me and how happy she was to be with me.

27 January

> You have only just now dropped me off, and already I feel your absence. When I think about building a home and life with you, it makes me giddy with happiness.
> I won't lie, it scares me too. I guess the more invested one becomes, the greater the stakes are, and the more one has to lose. You have far surpassed my expectations of what a good man is, and you have become the single most important thing in my life. It wasn't lost on me your effort to abseil down a mountain over the weekend. I know that is not your usual choice of activity, and you were in some way making an effort to immerse yourself in my interests in extreme activities. I do feel though, that perhaps you had an ulterior motive, and that is that you feel the need to compete with Marco, knowing that we used to do things like that all the time. I only say this, because it was easily sensed that you were not enjoying yourself and you were out of your comfort zone. You need to know that I fell in love with you 6 months ago for a reason. In fact many, many reasons, but the biggest reason was because of your great

qualities, none of which correlate to Marco. You are completely different people.... Thank God!!! So I ask you, sweet man, that from here on in, we choose to do things together that we both can enjoy, and build our own pool of memories. Deal? I love you so deeply and cannot wait to be with you tomorrow night. Sleep tight 10.24pm

28 January

Good morning!!! Well what a message!!! Sorry for responding late ... Slept in!! This message is so beautiful Simone. I know that U love me. We shall build a world together. Full of happiness and love , and laughter. I know that it was immature to book the abseiling for the reasons that I did, but I actually enjoyed the experience a little. U can't understand the feeling I had and have when something or somebody comes between us. I hope that I can describe it better when we talk later, and yes I want to be in your arms and inside u, because when we make love, we have a connection that is truly unique !!! Xoxoxo speak later Bella xoxoxo 7.33am

Waking up and reading this makes me feel so loved and thankful!!!!!! Can't wait for dinner tonight. Lets talk about everything then? ♡♡ 7.38am

TWENTY-SEVEN

31st January - Day 196

The 'Conference'

We started the week intending to spend a few nights together. Simone reminded me that I had suggested we have a trial week together to see how it would feel. On Monday however she had developed a sore throat and a slight fever. She said it was from the abseiling day, when she had caught a cold, and I knew she wasn't lying because the conditions were really quite terrible. She was better by Wednesday and stayed with me.

Suddenly, I realised that her trip to Singapore was that Friday. Was she really going? Was she creating another excuse and lying? I knew I had to get to the bottom of it, and I knew this time I would find the truth.

She asked me on Friday if we could have lunch and of course I agreed. She said she was due to fly out of Sydney in the afternoon with the rest of the office. So, I met her for lunch and over salad and coffee we talked about the conference and how eager we would be to see each other again. We talked about Peta's party which would be on the Sunday she was due to return as we had bought a present together and both looked forward to giving it to her.

But what she didn't know was that I had started an investigation into the truth. As I sat and looked at her and looked into her eyes, she did not know that I had already discovered that Singapore was a lie.

In my line of business I meet a number of professional investigators. One had become a friend over the years and occasionally I had asked for favours. In this particular case, I had rung him during the week. I explained the situation to Charles and he was very quick on the uptake.

"Michael this is a very familiar story and I can easily make some enquiries and find out what's going on" he said.

I asked him to do it and to do it quickly.

Charles, my own special Private Eye, was on the 'job'.

So, as I sat with Simone, talking about Singapore, its climate, the hotel she'd told me she would be staying in, I already knew it was one great lie. What I was really hoping was that she would tell me the truth as I probed and asked more and more about the conference.

I was hoping and praying for her to turn around and say: "Michael it's not true. I'm not going to Singapore. I made it up and this was the reason why..."

But it didn't happen. The atmosphere over lunch was quite surreal. It was almost as if I was viewing her from a distance yet we were only inches apart. I looked into her eyes and when she looked back they seemed hollow, evasive and devoid of emotion.

We said our goodbyes and kissed.

"Don't worry I will be back in just a few days", she said. With that I left and walked back to my office. The phrase 'a heavy heart' seems somewhat of a cliché until you actually experience it yourself. I could physically feel the pain of a love that was wounded. This time I knew it was terminal.

What followed after that seemed quite bizarre and added to the sense of unreality and detachment.

I received a series of texts late in the afternoon and I played along with my responses.

31 January

> I love you and miss you already. It will be a long week without you.
> ♡ ♡ ♡ Just got on the plane. We had a slight delay, but getting ready for take-off, so will switch off now.
> 1.24pm

> Have a wonderful and safe flight X
> 1.25pm

> Technology huh?!!!! Wifi on planes... what next??? They have some great movie choices, but all of them are the ones we've discussed seeing, so I'll wait till I get back and watch with you. Xoxoxo
> 1.28pm

> What a surprise!! how is the flight?? what time do U think u will land ? X
> 1.29pm

> I'm not a sci-fi fan, but Sandra Bullock is fantastic in Gravity. getting in late...2am your time. I'll call when it's a decent hour your time. I miss you so much already!!!!! ♡ ♡ ♡
> 1.49pm

> When does conference start???
> U will need to rest. Try and get
> some rest!! Did u eat some
> dinner?? Xoxo
> 8.12pm

> Watched the film, had some
> salad and now ready for bed.
> Conference starts at 9am. I will
> dream of you, and us and our
> future....night. Love you
> 9.15pm

> Good night get some rest I will
> call u in the morning. I love u 2 !!
> ♡ ♡ ♡
> 9.16pm

I liked her comment about the WIFI. It made sense she could text. I played along, knowing all the time, that this was a deliberate fabrication. Charles had rung me in the afternoon and confirmed the details of what I already knew. There was no conference in Singapore. He had also checked the whereabouts of her boss, and he was still in Sydney and planned to be there the whole weekend and into next week. There was no booking at the Novotel under any name. I played along with the charade even asking her how her boss was on the flight. She said she was lucky not to be sitting next to him because she had heard that he snores! An interesting comment, I thought!

That night I wondered where she really was. I knew that Marco had to be involved. Were they really in Singapore? Or had she flown somewhere else to be with him?

I reached the conclusion that she had actually flown out of Sydney so as I went to bed I had no idea that the next morning providence would intervene in a way I could not possibly have foreseen.

My last thoughts before I dozed off amused me: had my life really become a B-grade Hollywood melodrama?

My morning routine gave me some solace; I went for a run down to the park and was proud of my efforts to push my fitness levels to new heights over the last few weeks. Exercise was keeping me sane and controlling my anxiety and tension. I texted to my friend and 'interpreter' Peter, and suggested we catch up for breakfast at our usual spot. He agreed and we set the time for 11.30am. I showered and shaved and then walked towards his apartment thinking over and over the same thoughts that seemed trapped in my head. They were aggravated by the receipt of a text from her accompanied by a photograph of a conference hall full of people.

1 February

Hello and Good Morning!!! just walking out the door for the conference. Will try and contact you in the break. Hope your

weekend is going well. Say Hi to your daughter when you catch up later today.
11.09am

R u well??? How was Andrew on the plane??? Did he flirt???
Hahaha
11.14am

I was lucky enough to be seated elsewhere thanks to self-seating. Apparently he is a terrible snorer, so I managed to avoid that. Hahaha,
11.25am

> How's Novotel, hope it's not a
> dump!! Xoxox
> 11.26am

It's fine. Nicer than expected.
Turning phone off. Let the
boredom begin!!!! Seminar
starting. Any exciting plans
today? miss you!!!! xoxoxo
11.27am

> Great, have fun, speak later ... X
> 11.31am

This time last week, I was in
heaven, now I'm in hell. check
out my environment...
11.49am

The photo Simone had sent seemed very familiar... And then I remembered... I had seen all her photos in the iPad and this one seemed familiar because of the screens at the end of the hall. They were presentation screens at the front of the room and I noticed how they stood out with their electric blue colour. She told me weeks before that this was a seminar she had gone to many years ago. Now she was using this photograph to try and convince me she was actually attending a conference!

I met Peter and we started walking towards our favourite coffee shop down at Elizabeth Bay. I told him about my last 24 hours and he could not offer any explanation other than shock at the level of deception that seemed to be taking place. We walked for about 15 minutes and were due to turn left to head down to the Bay. I seemed however to be gripped by a magnet. I couldn't explain it. We were only one street away from her apartment block and I was drawn to it as if some force, some voice was telling me to walk past her building.

"Peter, let's go another way, I just want to walk near her place" I said.

Peter thought I was crazy but indulged me and followed. We walked around the corner, up the slight incline and her building came into view.

At that exact moment I saw an image that shook my soul to its very core. As I looked towards the entrance of the building, I saw two people emerging from the front door. These doors were glazed and led to the elevator in the lobby. They were both about 25 metres away but I knew the slender outline of the woman and her walk. The man with her was tall, slim, and blond. I stood there frozen. Peter actually kept walking and then realising I had stopped turned around and looked at me quizzically.

"What's the matter?" he asked.

I was speechless and couldn't respond. I simply pointed. Peter's gaze followed the direction of my finger and we both saw it was her.

We moved silently to the side of the road to shield us from their vision. As they got closer there was no mistake about this. I had seen his picture a thousand times. Simone and Marco were coming out of the building together. He was carrying flippers and wearing shorts and thongs. She was similarly dressed. It seemed clear they were off to the beach. As they walked past we had stepped back into a driveway and we watched in silence.

I looked at the expression on her face. I will never forget it. She was looking down, trance-like and appeared to be in pain. He seemed oblivious and was smiling. They were not talking as they walked past.

I remember my first reaction after the sheer initial shock passed. I looked up into the sky and said 'thank you God'. I don't know why I said it, but the feelings that I was trying to express were simple. I just wanted to acknowledge finally, irrevocably, that I had concrete proof that this was the most despicable deception. It was no longer inference or circumstantial evidence. I had seen with my own eyes that she was with him. Peter asked me if I was okay.

"Let's go and sit down. I really need to have a coffee. I wish it could be something stronger" I said.

We did that but I didn't talk much, I was still literally in shock.

Peter said he couldn't believe it either. Simone had seemed so sweet and we had seemed like the perfect couple. It was getting to be too much for me to bear.

"I think I'd prefer to be alone, I need to process this, and honestly, I'm on the brink of crying" and with that I bid my farewell and walked back to my apartment.

I had pain in my stomach, even though there was now a sense of profound relief that I knew what was happening, I couldn't mask the physical reaction. I got home and collapsed on the bed. For a few moments I thought I was going to be physically ill, but I pulled myself together and contemplated how best to play out this last scene.

Should I send her a message? Should I call her? I decided that I would wait a little and just ride out the sickness that I was feeling. I wanted to get over the shock and at least have the benefit and presence of mind to be able to be decisively coherent in the event we were going to speak.

And as was always the case, choice seemed to be denied to me by circumstance. My phone rang and it was her. She seemed happy to talk to me but could immediately sense from my voice that something had fundamentally changed. I asked her for her room number at the Novotel so I could ring her that evening. It's probably the way I asked, but she knew that I now knew... Suddenly the phone dropped out.

1 February

> Damn phone dropped out.
> Can u call immediately?
> I need to tell u something?
> 4.11pm

The last time I had asked Simone to call me immediately was when I had seen the photo of her and Marco on the platform for the bungee jump in New Zealand. At that time her response was immediate, but today I heard nothing.

Over an hour passed. Suddenly I could see that she was typing a message. The wonders of technology – real-time deception! The

> I know you know I'm not in Singapore....
> I am truly a fool. I'm not sure why I felt I couldn't tell you the truth? and the truth is....I cancelled at the very last minute due to my eating disorder. It's a demon that continues to torment me. I should be able to discuss this with you, but I get so embarrassed, and I'm ashamed at myself too for not being strong enough to fight it.
> I need to also be truthful about something else,
> Marco arrived last Wednesday, and I arranged to see him.
> Perhaps you speak an element of truth when you say I'm not over him nor him me. I know you are the love of my life, but perhaps there is something inside me stopping myself from being with you 100%.
> I hate myself for lying to you. I am not worthy of your love. This is a pretty good indication that I'm not the one for you. You deserve to be treated like a King,

minutes drifted past and she was still typing... I knew what the

235

message would say before it even arrived: –

> and I have treated you like dirt. I am so sorry... Stay away from me please. It's better for you.
> 5.31pm

I thought long and hard about my response. I wanted to be decisive, but at the same time I was being torn apart emotionally. So I typed:

> I have never met a more despicable person than u in my life, even in your confession u r still lying through your teeth!! There is no conference, I checked. Andrew is in Sydney this weekend and will be here all week. There was never a booking at the Novotel. But the whole lie came home to me at about 1 pm today I saw u both coming out of your building.
> I was with Peter. U have lied to me for months.
> I cannot believe a word u have said. I have put your things in a box and will send them to your office. I want the ring back because I gave it with profound love. A love that u have turned into excrement.
> It has no place in my life now. U r right about one thing, I do deserve so much better. Don't worry I won't knock on your door, I am not at all interested in meeting Marco.
> 5.58pm

TWENTY- EIGHT

3rd February - Day 199

Destiny

The rest of my weekend was a blur. I had to wrestle with the physical pain in my stomach and lack of sleep. No matter how many times one experiences a broken heart you can never really be ready for the pain and grief, the feeling of emptiness and the loneliness that wraps itself around your body and holds you prisoner.

You try to wrestle free but the thoughts and memories drag you back every time. It's a process which takes weeks, sometimes months before the anguish subsides. I hated the fact I would have to endure this. I hated that my perfect love story had turned out to be a mirage. I hated that I had lost control over my mind and that it would involuntarily return to chapters and memories Simone and I had shared. I couldn't control it and that drove me crazy.

On Monday morning I tried to make some sense of work but my brain simply wouldn't function. I was able to organise some external client visits which got me out of the office. I wanted to get her out of my life. I had packed her belongings the previous evening into a box and brought them to work. This was a painful emotional exercise. Seven months of my life had been reduced to a couple of dresses, a negligee, some cosmetics and her hair dryer. I also packed some cards that she had written and the key ring. Looking back now, I'm not sure if it was intentional that I got the half of the message that said...'THE JOURNEY ENDS' and Simone got the half 'WHERE LOVERS MEET'... Now everything seemed laced with double meanings. I didn't know what truth was anymore, but I did know, from this moment forward, the journey had indeed ended.

Even though I had told her on the weekend I would send her stuff to her office, I sent her a message asking when I could meet to give back her things, I wanted to say goodbye in person. She responded immediately and said that she was walking down past my building to deliver documents for a client and could stop by. I agreed to meet her and walked downstairs.

3 February

> Simone I have your things. I want to drop them off to u. I would also like the ring back as I said. It would be nice say goodbye.
> 9.55am

Walking to Angel Place now.
9.55am

> Can we meet for a minute please I can give u your things.
> 10.33am

When?
10.34am

> I have some free time before
> 11.30
> 10.35am

I'm heading your way now.
Please let me explain some things to you.
I stuffed up.....big time, I know that.
But there are circumstances I'd like you to hear about, u know I love you!!
10.36am

> I will meet u downstairs in 5
> 10.36am

My heart was in my mouth again. I thought this will be the last time I would see her, and I should remain dignified and not get emotional. The last message to me before she left her office seemed to imply that once again she wanted to explain the situation. Something in me stirred at the possibility that there could be an explanation, that maybe, just maybe there might be hope. I reprimanded myself. What a fool I was to even entertain these thoughts.

I stood in the street and waited for Simone to appear, and then I saw her. The agony on her face was palpable and my heart sank again. She saw me but couldn't keep her head raised for more than a second as she crossed the road. I suggested that we step next door into the coffee lounge. She started crying and her words made no sense.

She started to gasp almost fitfully and I still couldn't understand what she was saying. People were looking in our direction and I thought to myself that this was not the sort of goodbye I had been thinking would be appropriate.

"Listen, what are you doing at five?" I asked.

She said that she had arranged to meet a friend to talk about what had happened.

"If you care anything about me rearrange that and meet me outside my building at 5.00pm" I said.

She agreed and left. I sat there thinking what have I done? Why didn't I just give her back her belongings and be done with it?

I went back to the office and realised that I had one more appointment that day at 4 o'clock. Time dragged and my head was still spinning. I couldn't concentrate and mercifully my 4 o'clock rang and cancelled.

So I left the office at 3:45pm and decided to wander down to my favourite café to read the newspaper. I would grasp any excuse to take my mind off the situation.

This café was behind my building in Pitt Street and in my opinion served the best coffee in town. However as I walked in, I saw another customer take the last newspaper to his table and it looked as though he was digging in for a long session. I turned around and thought I would head back to the other café where I had been earlier that day with Simone. They had no shortage of newspapers and I just wanted to escape.

I was walking up Bent Street, literally only metres from the entry to the café when suddenly I saw a tall well-dressed figure coming towards me...blonde hair, blue eyes. I looked at his face and new instantly that I was staring right into the eyes of the one and only... Marco.

I simply couldn't believe that in a city of five million people, this man, my nemesis, was walking straight past me in a city street. Twice in 48 hours providence had delivered an opportunity for me to finally learn the truth.

Within seconds we were literally inches apart. I turned my head quickly and looked directly at him.

"Marco" I said. He spun around with complete surprise, looked at me quizzically and waited for my next move. I leaned towards him with my hand held out,
"Marco, it's Michael, Michael Sherman."

His instinct was to shake my hand, but the expression on his face indicated that he wasn't sure who I was. Perhaps he was thinking he had met me at some business function.

"It's Michael, Michael Sherman" I repeated, giving him the opportunity to register who I was.
"Don't you know the name?"

"No, no, who are you?" he replied in a thick Italian accent.

"Don't you know the name Michael?" I asked again. "No" he said curtly and suddenly his body language

braced with tension. "Is this some sort of joke?" Seemingly only on me I thought.

I knew I needed to defuse this immediately, so I stood back and said: "Friend, this is no joke" and I added one word, "Simone"

"Simone? What do you mean Simone? What has she got to do with this?"

Now I had his full attention.

"Didn't she tell you about me? Didn't she tell you about Michael? Michael Sherman?" I asked, thinking at some stage it was going to sink into this good-looking knuckle head.

"What are you talking about?" he responded, still remaining clueless.

I suddenly knew that email in relation to the Chinese wedding held the key to this mystery. He did not know who I was because he had never been told about me. So I drew breath and I said in a slow deliberate and restrained voice

"Marco, I know this is going to come as a shock to you but I've seen your face a thousand times in photographs. That is how I recognised you in the street."

I paused and then said slowly, with emphasis:

"I have to tell you that I have been in a close, personal and intimate relationship with Simone for the last six months."

Suddenly his whole body language dramatically changed. He slumped forward.

"What?? What are you saying??" he said with disbelief. "Let's go into the café and sit down and we can talk

about this" I suggested.

"Of course, of course" he agreed, but I could see that my last words had fractured him.

The confident young businessman striding down thestreet only seconds before was not the person who was now sitting slumped in front of me.

The next 45 minutes were possibly the most dramatic of my recent life. And, if I was any judge of character, I would dare say that it was also an extraordinary moment for Marco. He said he needed to make a quick phone call to cancel his appointments. He did this with clinical precision, and then sat down. I then calmly recounted what had happened over the last seven months.

He had had no idea... He told me he had been with Simone for eight years and that they were making a life together. She had hated Singapore and had decided to come back earlier to Sydney to find a job and organise their accommodation. He had planned to return to Sydney in March and they were to resume their cohabitation.

I told him that I knew about the Tahiti trip and the trip to Italy and the return trip via New Zealand. I also told him I knew about his affair with an Italian girl some three years earlier, and that Simone had told me that was the beginning of the real end to their relationship.

He looked at me in total amazement. He was bewildered and almost disorientated. He then began his account interspersed with comments, such as, 'Oh my God, I don't believe this', or 'This is the worst day of my life'.

Within a few minutes, as strange as it may seem, we forged a bond based upon our mutual deception. Then he told me his side of the story and for the first time, with each revelation I shared his feelings of shock from a short time before.

To gain his complete trust I showed him a number of photographs of Simone and myself together. I also gave him my business card which disclosed my position as legal counsel in a major corporation.

I wanted him to know that I held a senior position as it reaffirmed the integrity of the moment.

When I had told him that I knew of his affair with the Italian girl, he told me that he had never slept with her. He had only kissed her and he had confessed immediately to Simone. He said she had never forgiven him and would often raise it to chastise him. He told me how she had gone through the rubbish to find love letters. This was consistent with her account to me. I wondered if she had been honest with him in disclosing the two affairs she had embarked on after her little discovery. I wondered if she had ever been honest with him and disclosed the two affairs she had embarked on after her little "discovery". She had told me about these affairs on her first trip to Sydney.

He continued with a recollection of his life with her over the previous six months. They had planned the Tahiti trip together for months and she had planned independently to come to Sydney where she had already arranged interviews for a new position. Her text proclaiming that he had just turned up was a complete lie.
Now I was beginning to feel sick.

He had come backwards and forwards to Sydney over the past few months and this seemed to account for her erratic behaviour and mood swings. It explained why she suddenly had to leave on a Sunday morning or couldn't stay on a Friday night. It explained the endless texts and emails and phone calls.
But the explanation that really shook me to the core was when he looked up at me and said:

"What are you talking about? We never went to Italy. I came to Sydney to be with her at Christmas. We had planned the trip to New Zealand in early January, months before."

I had believed her that she had returned home to see her mother. I suddenly thought of myself sitting in her little flat giving her the present for her mother when I said goodbye before Christmas. I felt sick in the stomach again. Then I finally asked him the question over which I had been agonising.

"Marco, I have to ask you this man-to-man. Have you been intimate with Simone in the last six months?'

"Of course," he said both dismissively and indignantly.

He looked at me as though I was stupid. That stung me.

We both sat in silence with our heads down and in complete shock.

I went on to tell Marco about the whole Singapore conference ruse.

"I don't know whether you believe in God", I said, "and for that matter I don't know whether I do either, but there must be a reason why we met today. There must be a reason why I saw you two together on Saturday morning when she was supposedly in Singapore."

He explained to me that she had told him that she was in Hong Kong the weekend we had been in the Blue Mountains.

I soon realised that for every lie that she had told me, there was a perfect counter-lie that she had told him; the two dove-tailed with such precision that I was actually in awe of her Machiavellian ability.

"In my opinion", I said, "We have to end this nightmare immediately."

I told him I was meeting Simone at 5.00pm and I suggested we have a confrontation with her that afternoon. He agreed. I told him I would walk down to the ferry and we would go back to my place. I gave him the address and said to be there at 5.30pm. He agreed and gave me his card with his number.

He left and I just sat there.

TWENTY- NINE

Later that afternoon

The Set Up

I was still taking in what had just happened. The enormity of this deception was just starting to hit me. I felt sickened again in the stomach. I also felt, strangely, somewhat proud of myself in the way that I had dealt with Marco. It was 4.55pm and the adrenaline was racing through my body.

Like clockwork Simone appeared at 5.00pm and we walked to the ferry wharf hardly saying a word.

I noticed Simone was wearing the ring that I had given her. I was truly in awe of her duplicity but knowing what was about to happen, I somehow tingled with a feeling of delicious anticipation.

It was a reaction that I failed to completely understand, considering the hurt that I had suffered. Perhaps it was an unconscious satisfaction that her deception was being returned.

"I promise you everything will be resolved this afternoon", I said with complete sincerity.

She smiled at me and I thought to myself: "If only you knew what I now know!"

We boarded the ferry knowing that this journey was not the start of a long, lazy, romantic weekend as we had done in the past. We made small talk. I said to her that we would discuss everything in detail at home.

On the ferry I suddenly started to think a few paces ahead of the frenetic chain of events that had occurred in the last two hours.

What was I? Some sort of idiot? What was I thinking? I have

invited a perfect stranger to my apartment with the woman who he now regarded as his unfaithful partner.

What if there was a violent argument? What if she tried to run and jump off my balcony? These sorts of problems I didn't need. So once home, I was able to go to the bathroom where I quickly texted Marco and suggested that we should instead meet him at the park not far from her apartment in 20 minutes. He texted back immediately and agreed.

"Simone let me change quickly and we can go for a walk."

I laughed it off by adding: "You know me; I talk better when I walk and it's such a beautiful day. We can sit and discuss this whole matter."

She agreed and within minutes we were walking down the road. Once again I said slowly and deliberately,

"Don't worry; I know this will be resolved completely this afternoon."

Simone looked at me but didn't react.

I started to talk to her about the Singapore deception. I asked how could she be with him for a whole week and then return to me on Sunday to go to Peta's party?

She told me that she couldn't talk to him anymore and they were not sleeping together. I couldn't get the picture of his face out of my head when I had asked him exactly 'that' question and he had replied so indignantly, "Of course".

We walked past the yacht club and turned right towards the park. I noticed that I was unusually calm, strangely calm in fact.

I knew that in a matter of minutes Simone would be plunged into the total reality of her deception.

I saw the outline of a figure sitting on the sea wall with his back to us. It was him. She was oblivious to the people around us, almost trancelike and kept walking. As we passed him I looked back over my shoulder and could see the look on his face. The nightmare reality of what I had told him only an hour earlier was now there before him to see.

I thought to myself that perhaps he was reacting in the same way that I had reacted just that Saturday before.

We found a bench to sit on and she just sat staring ahead. There were tears in her eyes and they had been there all afternoon, threatening to fall. With my right arm I gestured to Marco to start his approach. I turned to her at that moment so there would be no mistaking what my words meant.

"I don't know whether you have ever read the bible Simone, but I believe there is a passage there that says: – "As you sow, so shall you reap." I want you to always remember these words when you think of this moment."

She looked at me and then looked up. He was standing over her. Her jaw dropped.

"Marco" she gasped as he sat down next to her.

I took the opportunity to launch into a monologue, they were both stunned.

"I don't know how this could have occurred; I don't know whether you believe in fate, but freakishly, I ran into Marco this afternoon in the city. I introduced myself to him and we sat down and had a talk. He didn't know me Simone." I paused. "He had never heard of me, and we talked for almost an hour. I now know everything... everything!'

I paused again for breath.

She burst into tears and looked at him.

"I tried to tell you... I tried to talk to you, but you never listen" she said accusingly, as if it was his only his lack of attention that lead her down a path of infidelity the past several months. "What do you mean I never listen?", and so it began; the conversation they should have had a year ago.

After all I had been through with her it now seemed to all boil down to me being in the middle of a domestic dispute.

Suddenly she got up and started to run, he immediately chased her. I didn't have the inclination or the energy to run after either of them, and strangely I felt as though they deserved some privacy.

They were about 25 metres from me and although I couldn't hear what they were saying I could certainly tell by the expressions and body language that it was a gut wrenching exchange.

I walked up to them and he turned to me and said, "We want to go back to our apartment" He was flustered, and his cheeks were blazing red.

"That's fine," I said, "I will walk with you, if that's ok. We can have a quick chat and I will go."

Simone was visibly shaking as we walked. I felt her hand slide into my pocket. I quickly felt inside the pocket and found the ring that I had given her. She obviously didn't want him to see it, and with that one action, she confirmed in my mind, the deliberate and surreptitious nature of her personality and the deceit which was the only currency she knew.

We walked back to her building. It only took about ten minutes and as we approached it I noticed her legs becoming wobbly and suddenly she fainted. I was able to catch her fall and Marco also supported her back. Passers- by ran over and offered help, water and ice. Marco remained silent, and left it to me to thank the concerned strangers for helping his girlfriend. I made some feeble excuse about the probable cause being heat exhaustion. We were eventually able to revive her and she staggered back to the apartment.

She lay on the bed and I fixed a cold washcloth for her head. I had a glass of water and sat down. He sat on the bed in silence. It was somewhat awkward for a few minutes until I could stand it no more. I stood up and spoke, breaking the tension.

"Simone, you now have to take responsibility for everything that you have done. I will never know or understand why you did it but what has been done cannot be undone". Marco also seemed to emerge from his trance-like state.

He looked at me and said:

"Michael, I understand what you have said today and I believe that you are honourable. You have handled the situation with dignity, but Simone and I need to be alone to talk."

"That's fine, I am not hanging around", I said.

At that moment I felt a crushing weight bare down my shoulders and as I turned to leave, the stark reality hit me: I was going home to an empty apartment. I was leaving her with this man who seemed so cold and distant towards her. My head was still spinning.

THIRTY

4th February - Day 200

No man's land

The walk home refreshed me. There was a cool breeze and the tension that had built up over the last two hours seemed to dissipate with every step.

But despite that I felt so sad, empty and profoundly lonely.

No matter how hard I tried, I could not hate Marco. I felt incredibly sorry for him and even pitied him. I remembered him at the café, how he kept repeating 'Oh my God, Oh my God this is the worst day of my life'. He could not believe this story, but I knew it was true.

My mind turned over the detail of our brief exchange, as if it had been filmed and I was watching a replay. I could review his every comment. I remembered him telling me about his impression of certain events and moments.

When I asked him, for example: "Do you remember when you got back to Sydney after New Zealand?"
He had replied: "Yes, we came back on the Thursday and I had to leave again on the Sunday to go back to Singapore".

I was still putting the pieces together, the pieces of this incredible puzzle and this labyrinth of lies. He said he couldn't understand her urgency to walk that afternoon as he got into the taxi. He remembered she took off like a bullet after she said goodbye and I told him, of course, she was racing to Double Bay to meet me.

I asked about that afternoon in New Zealand after the bungee jump. He said he remembered her mood swinging violently and how depressed she was. She put it down to the camping conditions. But I knew it was after I had had the screaming argument with her and told her how violated I had felt after she had lied to me.

My mind also returned tentatively to their sexual relationship. I honestly didn't feel that outraged that they were still sleeping together. She had lied about that of course, and had always assured me that my technique as a lover was vastly superior to his.
Now, however, I felt repulsed by these assurances.

So that evening I sent him a text asking how he was coping. He said that things had returned to some normality and yes everything was in order and they had gone for a walk. I suggested that we meet for coffee the next day so I could hand over her things, and he agreed.

Once again I resigned myself to a sleepless night; a night of tossing and turning and wondering 'what if?' Trying to work it out, trying to come to terms with the fact that the woman I was in love with had turned out to be a sick, lying, conniving wretch.

I wanted to hate Simone with every fibre of my being, but couldn't. My love was still too raw to hate, the shock too recent to even understand.

So the next day Marco and I had pre-arranged to meet for a coffee at 2.30pm. In the half crazed state of mind that I was in I completely forgot to bring the bag containing her possessions!

So our coffee talk was more general. I was hoping he would adopt the same candour he had exhibited the day before. We had both been duped and this had given birth to a strange sense of camaraderie.

But no, his guard was up again, and he had regained his composure. There was now something cold about him, in fact, every criticism that Simone had levelled at his callous lack of empathy, seemed to be highlighted now. Not that I really blamed him. Both of our lives had been impacted by this woman and we were coping as best as jilted lovers could.

Perhaps his sense of detachment prompted me to show him one of the texts that she had sent me. I remember even questioning my own motives as I scrolled down to find it. Was it some form of revenge? Was it some strange way that I wanted to show him how much she had meant to me? Maybe there is some truth in both, but I did want to watch his face when he read it.

"I want you to read this so that you know what you are dealing with. It was the text that she sent me after the weekend at the mountains barely a week ago" and I handed my phone to him to read.

His face was expressionless and motionless for what seemed to be an eternity. Then, ever so imperceptibly, there was a slight grimace. I knew it was the sentence where she said the reason that she loved me the most was because I was nothing like him. He glared at me with cold eyes.

"I do not need to read these things" he said dismissively handing my phone back.

"I just needed you to see this so you would understand the level of deception I faced" I said simply. I think he got the message. And maybe it was a tad immature on my part but, c'est la vie; it was done.

We agreed to meet again on Saturday morning so I would be able to hand over her things in exchange for a number of items that I wanted returned.

That night out of the blue she texted me. The message, strangely, was in regard to Peta's birthday party which was that Sunday. I had completely forgotten that we had bought a joint present. It was really the last thing on my mind, and she was texting me asking whether I wanted it gift wrapped!

4 February

> Would you like me to wrap
> Peta's present?
> 5.46pm

> I think it would be a nice idea to
> buy a lovely bottle of wine to go
> with the decanter. I am happy to
> chip in. I'm not going, but I figure

> we had already bought the
> present together. Let me know
> either way. Thanks...
> 8.08pm

Then another rambling text...

> I get it. I have lost her trust...in
> fact everyone's trust. I am
> starting again with everyone...
> except you.. I get that. from
> here on in, I will endeavour to
> live my life with utmost
> honesty and integrity. I know
> you will view that with some
> kind of scepticism, as I
> would if I was in your shoes. I will
> never forgive myself for the
> abhorrent way I have treated
> you and hurt you. I know you
> don't believe a word I utter... I
> have your earrings to give back.
> Let me know where you would
> like me to drop them off to.
> 10.01pm

I sat in astonishment at what appeared to be her completely dysfunctional personality. I thought to myself that maybe she was losing her grip on reality. Maybe she never had it to start with.

> Where is Marco
> 10.04pm

Sitting beside me. He knows I'm texting you. No need to torture him by showing my texts and emails to you. Again... I'm sorry for what I did to you.

10.07pm

> Good. I don't want u contacting me behind his back. Please show him this text.
> U will never understand the damage u have done.
> U have never been able to explain to me why u lied and cheated. What did I do to deserve such treatment. U told me that I was the only true love in your life and the most important person in your life. All bullshit. All lies. And I wanted him to know.
> I only showed him one, I could have shown him more, but I like him too much to hurt him. I just wanted him to know the level at which I was deceived.
> 10.14pm

She also told me that she was going into therapy, as if that would be the panacea. He then sent me a message suggesting that it would be best if I didn't contact her any more. I was completely in agreement with that and confirmed that was my intention!

The dust was beginning to settle and I tried to get my life back in order, especially my focus at work.

THIRTY-ONE

8th February - Day 204

Prisoner Exchange

That week was extraordinarily hard. I tried to get through each working day but my mind kept wandering. I used the opportunity to go for long walks, with the drama of the last few months constantly replaying over and over in my mind.

It's amazing how a love affair can consume so much energy and it's as if my memory had shifted into an unhealthy preoccupation with every aspect of our relationship. Finally, the weekend came and on Saturday morning at the appointed hour I picked up her bag of possessions and walked down to the park. I could see the outline of his figure in the distance. We met as if we were in 'no man's land', the irony being that we were within view of her apartment and I knew she was watching us; I could feel it.

This was the third time that I had met him and now there was no shade of humanity upon his face. This was a business transaction to be completed. I greeted him and he coldly shook my hand. I suggested that we might sit down and even grab a coffee as there was a café just 50 metres away. He looked at me and without emotion said:

"No we don't have time; we are off to the beach, so let's get this over and done with."

Yes a transaction indeed. Then he abruptly said:

"By the way, there are two messages for you from Simone. Firstly, it is Peta's birthday today even though the party is tomorrow" Once again I was thrown by the disconnect between what had occurred and the sheer banal, almost irrelevant nature of the message.

"Secondly," he went on to say, "Call your parents!"

I looked at him in disbelief. That was it? We exchanged parcels.

"I just have one question, just one question... did she say why? Did she have any explanation?"

He looked at me and with the faint beginning of a smile and a slightly vicious tone in his voice said:

"It was just a bit of fun..."

To me this was a totally inappropriate cheap shot and I could not accept it. The three of us had been through hell over the last week and this was the first streak of spite that had entered the arena. Maybe he was just returning fire after I had shown him the text during our coffee?

I really don't need this, I thought.

With that said we were well and truly done, and I turned around and walked. I could feel her eyes drilling into the back of my head. I could feel her presence. And I thought to myself, will I look back at her apartment?

Another ten paces, will I look back? I thoroughly reprimanded myself; do not look back, do not give her the satisfaction of knowing that my heart had been smashed.

Whilst walking home I felt that something inside me had been broken. I prayed that it wouldn't take too long to heal because I really did not want to be in a state of emotional misery for months. I had been there before and I knew how wasteful of energy and time this whole process was. So I pledged to myself that I would summon up all my reserves of strength and character that I knew I possessed, and I would move forward and recover and heal as quickly as humanly possible. But most of all I vowed I would find someone who would never, never, lie to me again.

THIRTY-TWO

10ᵗʰ February Day - 206

Treatment

I thought I had come to the end of this extraordinary story. I thought that I would find peace knowing there would be no further contact between us ever again. But no sooner had Marco left to return to Singapore on that Sunday, the day after our 'prisoner exchange', a text arrived from Simone

10 February

> Hi, I'm sorry for contacting you. I want you to know that I've started seeing someone professionally, and am trying to process my actions. OMG I can only imagine the feelings you must have towards me. The feeling of complete deception and betrayal. Please believe me when I say, I NEVER lied about how I felt about you. But I also know, you can never believe a word I say......completely understandable. Marco and I are struggling to get through this

too. I have caused a lot of damage all round. I was hoping you would spare me a few minutes face to face, to give me a chance to explain. I understand if you never want to see me again....and yes Marco knows I was going to ask you for a meeting. No more lies will rule my life.
9:14 pm

She wanted to meet! She wanted to talk and, in truth, I wanted to talk to her too. So I sent a message to Marco telling him that she wanted to meet with me and he said he knew and had no concerns. How gracious of him. And so I arranged for her to meet with me on the Tuesday night after he had left. It would have been the first time that we had talked face-to-face in ten days.

I rang her that night to confirm arrangements.

11 February

I have just woken up. After we spoke on the phone, I fell into a deep sleep. Thanks for agreeing to see tomorrow. xoxoxox
1.02am

Morning, I slept in, and I didn't sleep all that well. I am so glad that we discussed these things last night, I think it is all part of your recovery. See u tonight xxx
7.21am

I cannot tell you how great it was talking to you again. I miss our chats and our texts. As soon as I finish work, I'll contact you. xoxo
7.22am

Ok xxx
7.23am

> I have had the worst day, extremely stressful. I'm running very late and missed the bus. I will jump in a cab.
> 6:07 pm

> Why not catch the ferry 6.27?X
> 6.12pm

> Won't make it. Cab will be fine.
> 6:14pm

> Ok .. Don't rush, I am here. xx
> 6.17pm

> On my way. There in 5mins
> 6.49pm

I couldn't believe we were texting with 'kisses' after what had happened. I was an addict and she was supplying my 'fix' again.

I wasn't sure what I would say to her so I just began with a stream of consciousness that built and built. It became quite a monologue and I even impressed myself as to my level of recall and the detail to which I was able to refer. I levelled every lie she had ever told me and put each one to her. She sat with her head down, shaking, and tears running down her cheeks.

"I hate what you did, but I just can't bring myself to hate you" I expressed this as sincerely as I could without too much emotion. She looked up. I had thrown her a lifeline. I didn't even realise what I'd said or the implications that could follow. I again swept over the facts that she had lied about everything, but before I got too far, she interrupted me abruptly.

"I promise you, I never lied about the way I felt about you" she told me.

"If you really mean that, then it would be so simple. All you had to do is tell him it's over and come to me, but your words and your actions are entirely disconnected, so frankly I just don't believe you"

I paused for a beat, "if you really meant what you said then I have two non- negotiables"...

I had thrown her not only a lifeline, but a first-class ticket to get back on board!! I couldn't believe that I was putting a reconciliation proposition to her, but I did and continued on...

"If you truly want me and you truly love me then you end it with him NOW, immediately and you get down on your hands and knees and beg forgiveness from all the people that you have hurt with your lies. This means my parents, my family and all my friends that you have hurt through your stupidity. And even when you've done that, I can't guarantee that I can ever open my heart to you in the same way that we were. But if you truly love me that's what you need to do."

I stopped there. There was nothing more to add, and I couldn't even believe I had put that forward. Did I really want to subject myself to a life of uncertainty with her? How could I possibly believe a single word that would pass over her lips? Perhaps what I really wanted was to win her over Marco. Was this simply unabashed, raw ego? I was acting and talking completely irrationally, but at the end of the day I had invested almost seven months of my life in her and I couldn't bear to see it end. Not yet and not like this.

She said she understood and she left.

You have no idea what that meant to me just now being able to see you and talk. Thank you..!!! Sleep well.Xo
9.54pm

Meant a lot to me too, sleep well too xx
9.55pm

Can't sleep. I feel a little lost and really need to hear my Mum's voice. I'm a little unsettled.
10.07pm

Maybe u should tell her a little about what is gong on??
R u ok? xx
10.10pm

As much as I want to and need to tell her, I can't. It will kill her. She didn't raise me that way. If she knew the level of deception I have been living in the last 8 months, she would be so disappointed, and I'm disappointed in my own actions enough, without disappointing someone else I love.
It cut me like a knife seeing the pain in your eyes tonight.
10.12pm

Also, Marco called. He asked how the meeting went. I am just letting you know so there are no more secrets. I want to be completely transparent.
10.13pm

I understand, I want u to resolve these things and I want u to be happy. I want u to know real love and that u can trust someone.
Xxx
10.15pm

I'd love that too!! Going to give mum another try. She was engaged before.
Night
10.22pm

Goodnight!! speak tomorrow. X
10.23pm

We talked over the telephone during the week. We made arrangements to meet for a walk after work. In the morning I received this text.

13 February

You told me last night that you were angry with yourself. I thought about those words all night. I can't believe that my stupid and thoughtless actions have caused you to feel that you are to blame. You have done nothing wrong. In fact the complete opposite.
You have been amazing....
even after the fact.
7.06am

Good morning, I am so happy that we are talking with complete honesty.
I know that it is part of the healing process. If we r honest we know there r still strong and powerful feelings that we have for each other . I know u have the strength to fight through this. I am prepared to stand with u.Xxx
7.19am

I'm not sure if I can even get through all this, but I feel I have been given another chance, and I'm not going to throw that away. I have to make the choices from now on, and I choose honesty. There will be nothing but honesty in my life from now on Michael!!
7.30am

U must not doubt yourself. You do have it. Believe it or not u r actually through the worst!!!
U see the world clearly now, not as an elaborate deception or game. This is your chance for real freedom and happiness. As u say grab it with both hands!!! Xxx
7.34am

The day passed slowly. Our usual daytime communication had understandably dropped right off, but she was never far from my thoughts.

U awake?
9.56pm

We spoke for half an hour. I was convinced that she was moving down the same path as me. She told me things I wanted to hear... needed to hear.

So began a tortuous, almost clandestine reconciliation.

I wasn't sure how much Simone was telling Marco, and quite frankly I couldn't give a damn whether she did or didn't tell him. The way we interacted together when we exchanged belongings left such a bad taste in my mouth, I knew I had no loyalty towards him, nor did I owe him any favours. My duties to him were fulfilled and it made my decision to pursue her that much easier.

There was something magnetic about Simone, something that was drawing me to her again. I knew I was a fool to even consider allowing her back into my heart, but it was an irresistible force and I couldn't control it. So we continued to meet and resume our walks and talks. I started to rebuild some basis for the trust that had been shattered. She kept telling me that all she could think about was me and how much she loved me.

"Well if this is true then your decision will be easy. But it is your decision, and I don't want to be seen as placing any pressure on you"

The weekend arrived again and I spoke to her on Saturday afternoon. She had been speaking with Marco and he must have told her that we were not to have any further meetings. She rang me and told me what he had said. I said that I needed to tell her that this was the bitter end and I didn't want any further contact with her if she was going to accept his instructions after what she had told me.

As I was informing Simone of my intention to terminate this relationship once and for all, she insisted on meeting me in the park, refusing to accept my decision. She begged me to be there as she had something "important" to say to me.

I was intrigued and so I reluctantly agreed. We met in the area that I had dubbed 'no man's land', on the exact bench that I had stood with Marco, only that last week when we had handed over each other's possessions.

I asked her why did she want to keep prolonging the agony and treating me with such disrespect, but alas, she had no answer. The best she could come up with in response was that he had some kind of power over her. I didn't buy it. I told her I didn't believe anything she said anymore, and that we really should consider whether there was any future in continuing this conversation. This whole catch up had been a fruitless exercise and one of which I was quickly growing tired.

"Think about it, I really don't want to stay" and with that, I took my leave.

As I walked home, the anger was slowly building in me. Why did I subject myself to this? Why did I continue to build such false hope? Why couldn't I let go? I couldn't answer any of these questions with a semblance of dignity.

No sooner had I returned home that I received another text.

15 February

> I'm outside your apartment. I need to ask you a final question, but I understand if you don't want to see me.
> 4.49pm

> Yes I will come up
> 4.50pm

I walked up to the front of my building thinking that this whole melodrama was now taking on a pathetic colour. I let her in and we walked down to my apartment. We sat on the couch.

"All right what is the question?" I asked wearily. She looked at me with begging eyes.

"Do you think I have the guts to get rid of him?" she said.

I thought to myself: "Is this the question?" I was actually quite disappointed.

"If you can't see that it's not what I think, it's what you do, then you just don't get it. This is not a game we are playing; I don't need to dare you to drop him. You can either summon up the courage to do it, or you can continue to bullshit me. If it's the latter I am really getting bored."

I think she could tell by my reaction that I just didn't believe her any more. As she was leaving I left her with one final thought,

"You need to think about where you are and what you want to do and then we can talk."

I closed the door without a smile or a hug. I was close to feeling absolutely nothing now. I was close to throwing the towel in. This whole experience was draining my life force.

And it wasn't long after her visit the next text arrived

15 February

It took a lot of courage to come and see you tonight, so I thank you for allowing me some of your time. I have made a decision, and I am waiting to talk to Marco.
He is working and I've left a message asking him to call me back.
8:55 pm

THIRTY-THREE

16th February - Day 212

Second Chance?

Strangely during the next week we talked for hours on the phone. I tried encouraging her and telling her that she did have the courage, all she had to do was to press the button.

16 February

I finally got to speak with Marco. I was very open and honest with him and explained that I still care very deeply for you, and try as I might, the feelings won't go away. He too opened up, and told me things that I wished he had of told me a long time ago. In truth, I'm heartbroken to hear his revelations, but I have to remain true to myself. Never in my life have I suffered such emotional turmoil, and I have caused the whole dilemma. I'm not sure why I'm off-loading to you. I have put you through enough. I think it best if I take some time out and keep to myself and try and process what I've done and what I can do to fix it, and what I want for my future.

> The only thing I do know is without truth I don't have a future. Take care Michael.
> 4.31pm

> I wanted to have a quick talk to u
> 5:54 pm

Every time Simone made a decision to have time out to sort herself out, I felt compelled to talk to her. I just couldn't allow her to retreat in case I lost her forever. It actually made no sense. I should have been listening to her and taking on board her concerns, but she had become so addictive that the thought of her not being a part of my future was difficult to comprehend. I was fighting hard for something I truly believed in. In spite of everything she had done I was convinced that we had a chance of success. When things were right between us, it was magical. We were a formidable team. I needed to remind her of this. I called her. I wanted her to know I was there for her and was willing to support her through her therapy. Again she replicated my thoughts, concreting in my mind that our intentions were indeed travelling along the same path.

> Home, safe and happy. I want to dream the dream with u again, built on integrity and the truth. X
> 8.56pm

> I want the same thing, more than anything. How would you feel about seeing me after my therapy appointment this week, so I can keep you up to speed on what's happening and my progress updates. I'm going to call mum
> 8.59pm

273

Yes, I would love to come on Tuesday maybe I could pop in for 5 minutes
We can have a snack after ?? Xx
9.04pm

Wow, you'd do that? Let me ask her if that's ok tomorrow! Thank you x
9.05pm

R u going to tell your mother?
9.07pm

Little bits at a time. If I reveal the whole lot at once, she will be overwhelmed with worry.
9.08pm

Understand, does she speak any English?
9.10pm

lol...no, none. You will have to brush up on your Italian. XXX
9.11pm

Did u speak to her?
9.46pm

Just said goodbye 5 seconds ago. She is so supportive, and told me the encouraging things I needed to hear from someone who knows me better than anyone in the world.
She told me I'm stronger than I think, and she knows I will find happiness eventually. It breaks my heart to hear her talk so positively, when I know she lives in misery after my dad left her completely impoverished.
He stole her life away from her from the moment he asked her

> to marry him, and then robbed her of any happiness throughout their marriage by being a violent drunk, and then stole all their savings. He was a pig.. She hates that I support her financially, but I wouldn't have it any other way. I can't wait for the day when you finally meet her...X
> 9.50pm

> I would love to!! U r strong, and I am right beside u again sleep tight Xxx
> 9.52pm

> You too! xx
> 9.56pm

We went out for dinner on Tuesday night and went back to one of our favourite cafés. I said I brought her there because we had so many great memories at this place. These were happy times for us and frankly I was so tired of all the stress and anxiety, I just thought we could chill out there that evening and talk about some of the things that we did get right. It was sort of a truce and she really appreciated the gesture. Suddenly we both relaxed and were chatting as if it were the 'good old days'. We also started to text again, as if we were lovers but I was barely holding her hand and hadn't touched her for three weeks.

18 February

> Good morning. Hope u slept well... Xx
> 6.25am

275

Morning. Best sleep I've had in a week. How about you?
7.02am

I am sleeping with good thoughts for a positive future, a future that I invite u to share with me. With honesty and real love. The roller coaster has ended. It is now time to heal, and to open our hearts. X
7.05am

I am so very happy when I think of our future. But I can't pretend it doesn't petrify me at the same time. I have learnt a lot from my lies, and I vow to live with honesty and openness from here on in.
7.11am

Wonderful, let's begin the journey together and rebuild our trust and our passion and love. Don't be afraid!!! I want u to live a happy and wonderful life ... Xx
7.13am

As do I!!! xxx
7.26am

Hi, Hope u r feeling better? I will call later to say good night. Thinking of you xxx
8.05pm

We continued to talk on the phone each night and decided to go out for dinner, later that week on Friday. Although, I have to confess, that although I was building expectations, there was something strangely dull about my thoughts. I didn't know whether I could believe her and this took away an edge from my sense of commitment. I just thought to myself to 'go with the flow' as they say and listened to her and believed once again her continued proclamations of love.

19 February

> Good morning, how did u sleep?
> I bet your mind is swirling after yesterday!!!
> I had a lovely night. Remember every day is another little step forward to your future !!! Xox
> 7.37am

Morning, sleep was alright. A little restless I guess. I just have so many thoughts swirling around my head. I just have to trust that each day will get better, or easier. Thanks for last night. I had a great time, as I always do when I'm with you. Hope you slept well. Talk later
xxx
7.40am

> My mind is also swirling. I missed u last night. I really believe that ultimately u have to follow your heart. I always have.
> I believe that we met for a reason and our love was real and still Is!!! I believe that we are soul mates. Hope it is not too heavy first thing in the morning , but this is the most important thing in our lives !!! I believe that u will be true to yourself
> And I will be beside u!!!! Xx
> 7.47am

You nearly made me cry. What beautiful words to wake up to, thank you!! I feel the same, and I believe things happen for a reason. Although, that makes more sense regarding our meeting, than the atrocious way I have treated you and Marco. It's a long journey to recovering from this I'm afraid.
8.01am

I know, and there is no rush, I just want u to know I have opened my heart to u again. I want us to take the journey again! Xoxo
8.04am

Michael you are so incredibly kind to me. You are offering me a second chance with your heart after I crushed it. A lot of people wouldn't take that chance with something so vulnerable and precious. You humble me with this gesture.
Our journey will go on, but this time we will take an alternative route. XOXO
11.39am

But deep in my heart I knew there had been so much damage to my sense of trust; and that nagging suspicion that this was going to prove again to be an elusive mirage.

19 February

Tonight's discussion means the world to me. We r best friends you know that. It's so wonderful to talk to u freely and to tell u my

fears and how I feel. It's a 2 way street and I will support u with every ounce of my fibre, but I need u too!! And when u say that u never want to lose me my heart sings. I love u ♡
8.23pm

20 February

You are such a beautiful romantic gentleman. I want to tell you something tomorrow when I see you
9.17pm

I hope it is a good surprise!!!
9.17pm

Well... It not like you're facing a firing squad. let's say that. Xo
9.18pm

Hmmm ... Well I trust u ... X
9.19pm

I seriously hope so!!! I need you to feel that from here on in you can. Xoxo
9.20pm

Sleep tight sweetheart !! Xoxo
9.20pm

And you as well. I cannot tell you how much I'm in love with you.....
9.22pm

My heart is melting ... Xoxo
9.22pm

Good night
9.23pm

 Hey just like the old days.... ♡
9.23pm

Friday began with more texting and more importantly a sense that perhaps the nightmare of mistrust and suspicion was ending.

21 February

Good morning!! I slept in!! Hope u had a great night, so looking forward to seeing u tonight!!! So much to talk about .So much for us to do!!! Xoxo
7.01am

Morning. I'm excited to see you tonight.
Spoke with mum last night, she is holding something back from me. I'm worried, but I'm not privy to the whole story. Ill fill you in tonight. Have a great day.
7:21 am

Sorry to hear. Don't worry we can discuss tonight. Every problem has a solution, have a good day xoxo
7.23am

P.S. loved your message last night, brought back wonderful memories x
7.24am

Where are you?
10.10am

Gerringong, past Kiama.
So beautiful. It's a winery!!
Crooked River Winery.

280

Fantastic place! xx
10.22am

That's right you did tell me. I'm not sure how to tell you this, but I'm not feeling good. I am having serious panic attacks. I feel faint and sick at the same time. I'm thinking maybe it's best if we don't see each other until I'm fixed.
I need to be 100% right in order to be my best for you. Are you clear with what I'm trying to say?
12:52 pm

I rang her and tried to calm her. I began to feel that same sinking feeling I'd experienced only weeks before. In my heart I knew I was fighting a losing battle. I eventually persuaded her to come out to dinner with me and she accepted. I had a sense of foreboding and wondered whether this would be the last time I would ever see her.

We sat at our regular table at the Apollo Greek restaurant in Potts Point. I told Simone that I had a surprise for her.

On our visit to the Blue Mountains last November – just four months earlier – we had stopped in Leura. On this visit we had bought an elegant red leather-bound journal together.

I pulled out the journal and opened it.

Simone had previously recorded her thoughts on the first page. She had written: –

For Michael

You came into my life unexpectedly, and everything took a turn for the better. Your eyes, and a laugh, the sincere way you speak, and a kindness that you showed me, all became part of my life.

With every day, I discovered you more and more. I have never seen so much gentleness in one person. Without even knowing it, you are slowly making a place for yourself in my heart. It used to seem so hard at times to feel so close in a relationship. But it's so easy to feel close to you. I realise now that I had never known what it meant to be in love until I was loved by you. To live and to have someone special, someone who you can always depend to be there throughout the ups and downs, sharing laughter and tears as a partner, a lover and a friend.

I'm about to learn the full meaning of sharing and caring and having my dreams all come true, I've learned the full meaning of being in love, by being with you and loving you.

I love the way you touch me; it makes me tingle all over.

I love the way you kiss me. It starts a fire deep down inside of me and makes me yearn for you even more.

I love the way you look at me. It makes me feel beautiful and treasured. Most of all, I love the way you love me.

When you walk into the room, my whole day gets better. And even when you are not with me, you are in my thoughts always. It doesn't matter what we have or what we don't have. The most important thing is we have each other, and no one can that away. You and I are connected in a way that goes beyond romance, beyond friendship, beyond what I've ever had before.

I love you Michael, you have changed my life! Simone

I had read those words earlier that afternoon and in the cold hard light of recent events I felt that I was dealing with someone who was possibly mentally disturbed.

So I had written a note to her in reply. I read it to her now: –

I didn't know that you had always been afraid. I didn't know that you had never really loved.

I didn't know how hurt you had been. I didn't know how damaged you were.

I didn't know your pain and sorrow were your friends and that you were a prisoner in a house of lies.

But I know you now and I love you still… I love you because I know that you loved me when all was lost; I love you because you are fighting for me; I love you because you stood up for the first time in your life and said:

I will be free.

I will now choose to be happy.

I love you because you have the courage to love me.

Michael

Perhaps it was the inner lawyer in me but I also drafted a text that I wanted us to send to Marco and read it to her: –

As you know Simone and I have been in contact since last week. She has explained to you, despite all that is happening that she still has very strong feelings towards me. I must also acknowledge that those feelings are mutual. We both feel that we must work through these feelings and resolve them, for all our sakes. I'm very sad that these issues will hurt you, but we must all be honest and deal once and for all with this situation.

Michael

That afternoon I visited all the memories contained in this one little red book. What at the time was a scrapbook of the special memories of a burgeoning romance had now become a documentary testimony of misplaced love and affection. Inside were our tickets to La Bohème on 22 August, the confirmation of the Japanese restaurant on the Gold Coast on 23 November, the weekend when we went up to meet my parents, our welcome to the

Singapore hotel by the manager, our travel arrangements from Singapore back to Sydney in September, our trip to the Norman Lindsay Gallery and Museum in the Blue Mountains.

I guess I was trying to create the momentum for an irresistible bond between the two of us, and show her that despite all that had happened, we could still be the team that we had once talked about.

Over dinner we agreed that on Saturday Simone would ring Marco in Singapore and tell him simply and clearly that she wanted to be with me and she had to end their relationship once and for all, without any reservations.

After she had made the call we planned for her to walk to my apartment, and then we would cook a beautiful dinner together in the knowledge and celebration that we were really commencing a life together. After dinner we said that we would ring her mother in Italy and make the announcement.

Even I was starting to believe that this was no longer fantasy but a credible reality. After dinner at The Apollo we went for a walk down to Elizabeth Bay. We sat on a bench and I turned to her and kissed her. It was a long and luxurious kiss, and she kissed me back with passion. I walked back to her apartment and wished her a good night's sleep.

As I caught a taxi home, I sat with a sense of serenity that had eluded me for months. However, this peace of mind did not last and my thoughts raced as doubts swelled within me like dark clouds. The nagging question remained: Could I trust her? I would soon find out.

21 February

Safely home? xo
8.39pm

Good night my darling.
Dream dreams of happiness. Xo
8.48pm

What a lovely thing to dream about.
I'm so glad I ignored the stupid thoughts in my head and thank you for getting me to see sense.
Think I need to relay some things

to my mum. It's time to let her in, and hopefully she will expel some of my demons.
8:53 pm

Well that didn't go as well as planned.
In fact now I have caused another upset to another important person in my life, on the other side of the world.
There was nothing I could say to make her feel at ease about my situation.
I told her not to worry...but it fell on deaf ears. She was crying. I feel so far away. So helpless. Do you think you might speak with her? I think it would really help ease her mind.
Would you mind?
10.03pm

Good night!!! ♡
11:26 pm

I lay there. I did not reply. I just wanted to be alone.

285

THIRTY- FOUR

22nd February - Day 218

Goodbye

Saturday morning arrived and I woke with a burst of adrenaline-fuelled energy. I decided to go for a run and went down to the usual park near her apartment.

I had texted to wish her good morning and she had indicated that she too would go for a run. I thought it would augur well if we were to cross paths, and it happened exactly that way. So we decided to run a little bit together and then walked and talked and confirmed the arrangements again, and off she went.

22 February

I'm in Bondi grabbing a juice and checking out the markets. Lots of fresh fruit and veggies. What time are you seeing Naomi?
10:06 am

That's great! And so good for u! Yes am walking to meet her. Good luck with your Skype. Just be true to yourself.

Will be thinking of u xx
10.26am

I'm a little nervous I'll admit x
10.27am

Friday began with more texting and more importantly a sense that perhaps the nightmare of mistrust and suspicion was ending.

21 February

Good morning!! I slept in!! Hope u had a great night, so looking forward to seeing u tonight!!! So much to talk about .So much for us to do!!! Xoxo
7.01am

Morning. I'm excited to see you tonight.
Spoke with mum last night, she is holding something back from me. I'm worried, but I'm not privy to the whole story. Ill fill you in tonight. Have a great day.
7:21 am

Sorry to hear. Don't worry we can discuss tonight. Every problem has a solution, have a good day xoxo
7.23am

P.S. loved your message last night, brought back wonderful memories x
7.24am

Gerringong, past Kiama. So beautiful. It's a winery!! Crooked River Winery.

> Yes, I will channel my strength to
> u!! Xo
> 3.53pm

> XXX
> 3:53 pm

> Good luck...All my love is with u
> xoxo
> 3:55 pm

At 7.00pm I sent a message in a sense of frustration and anxiousness.

> Hi any news??? Xx
> 7.00pm

And then the text that I was dreading:-

> I have literally hung up just now.
> You are going to hate me... I
> couldn't do it. I'm so sorry
> Michael, I'm so sorry. My heart
> says yes leave him, but my head
> says no.
> 7:12 pm

Before her words could even sink in, she was ringing me. I answered she was crying uncontrollably.

"I couldn't do it; I couldn't do it, I'm so sorry. I am going back to him", she said.

My reaction shocked me. Somehow I knew in my heart of hearts that this would be the case.

"You don't have to go back to him; you were never away from him. Please don't ever contact me again, I'm tired of you playing with me and playing with my feelings" I replied wearily.

I hung up. This was the end, the very bitter end.

And so the story ends just as it began as a metaphor for life. Nothing is certain, nothing lasts forever, and the joy of the promise of love is so often overtaken by despair and grief that inevitably follows.

22 February

> I attach message I have sent to your boyfriend Marco ...U need to know that Simone has been contacting me all week and has told me that she is in love with me and wants to be with me. She told me that she is telling u these things. Last night we met and she again professed her love. We sat on a bench and kissed for half an hour. She has deceived me again, and cheated on u for the last time. I never want to see her or have any contact with her again. I do not trust a word she speaks. U can draw your own conclusions. I wish I had never met her. Michael
> Please don't ever contact me again.
>
> 8:20 pm

I often think about that beautiful vulnerable girl that I met on 'tango night' at the Crystal bar. I think about the zenith of our joy, and the depth of my despair upon learning of her deception.

And I think again about the small poem I wrote to her once, with a little help from William Shakespeare:

"The journey ends where lovers meet, provided there is no deceit.
Let hearts ring out and souls declare... You were my destination."

About the Author

J.D. Watt was born in Sydney, Australia. He has had a 30-year career in professional services and consulting. He served in the Armed forces, was the manager of a Rock 'n Roll band and a part-time lecturer at the University of New South Wales, Australia. He still lives in Sydney, Australia overlooking the magical Sydney Harbour.

Acknowledgement

First Edition Creative Contribution Fiona Mahl

First Edition Edited by Jeff Gilling and Fiona Mahl

Printed in Great Britain
by Amazon